16.95

TRICK OR TR

TRICK OR TREAT

LESLEY GLAISTER

BLOOMSBURY

JAN 1 8 2003.

First published in Great Britain by Martin Secker & Warburg 1991
This paperback edition published by Bloomsbury Publishing Plc 2002

Bloomsbury Publishing Plc, 38 Soho Square, London W1D 3HB

A CIP catalogue record is available from the British Library

ISBN 0 7475 5985 6

10 9 8 7 6 5 4 3 2 1

Typeset by Palimpsest Book Production Limited,
Polmont, Stirlingshire
Printed in England by Clays Ltd, St Ives plc

For Joshua with love

One

Olive sprawls upon the floor, for she suffers with her back, watched by Arthur, watching the tea-time news. It makes less and less sense these days. The confusion that fogs her brain has floated outwards from her, permeating the world; and it is reported back, on the BBC, at six o'clock and at nine o'clock.

People are fleeing and boundaries dissolving; people are missing and people are starving. People are popping in and out of orbit in model spaceships. There is danger in the food, danger in the water, danger even in the air, it seems.

'Need a pee,' says Olive. Arthur heaves his old bones off the giant leather chair where he perches, and stretches out his arm to Olive, who weighs seventeen stone to his seven.

'One of these days I won't manage this, me duck,' he gasps. Olive almost pulls him to the floor, grunting and heaving. She is beautiful to lie upon. Her thighs are as thick and solid as the arms of the old chair, her bottom the full seat's width, her belly an endless concertina of soft folds. But now she wobbles precariously upright, and Arthur collapses back into his chair.

Olive goes out to the yard. They have a bathroom upstairs but she only tackles the stairs at bedtime, and is just as happy in the outside lav. Kropotkin, the spaniel, nuzzles round her ankles as she lets her bloomers fall.

'Good lad,' she says. 'Good old Potkins.' Kropotkin lives in the outside lav since he cannot be trusted indoors. Indoors, with Olive and Arthur, lives Mao the bald cat. He was hit by a bicycle years ago and his fur fell out in a flurry of indignation and never grew back. He is an odd-looking beast and he needs pampering, for he feels the cold. At night, given half the chance, he snuggles into bed between Olive and Arthur, for all the world like an ancient, skinny baby.

When she's finished, Olive stands in the garden looking at the lights of the city spread out below her, glittering and fizzing under a stony moon. It is a mild night and the air is faintly orange, stained with street lamps and the tang of autumn smoke. This is the view that Olive has had for almost all of her eighty years. She grew up in this house, left only briefly, and returned after her mother's death. It became her own house then, bequeathed to her: Olive who didn't hold with private property, who never meant to stay. It was expedient, however, with the war approaching. She had to live somewhere, and there had to be somewhere for Arthur's return. But Olive never meant to stay, would never have believed, as a girl, that she'd end where she'd begun, with this same view spread out below her.

There is a noise. Kropotkin holds up his head, suddenly alert, and yaps. Olive stiffens. Someone is coming up the passage. She shuffles to the high wooden gate, unlatches it, and peers round its edge. She gives a little frightened moan.

It is a band of devils, crackling and black. They carry lamps, lamps that swing. One of them swings round and she sees a burning grin, a devil's grin. They are banging at the door. Olive closes the gate and leans herself back against it. Her heart is pattering deep in her chest and she struggles to catch her breath.

She hears Arthur open the door. She hears unearthly cackles and she hears the devil's voice. 'Miaow,' it says, but it is never a cat, it is a devil, masquerading. 'Trickortreat,' moan the voices and the devil/cat calls out again.

'Clear off,' says brave Arthur, and then she hears him gasp and shout, 'Clear off, hooligans!' and the door bangs, and there is the crackle and mirth of the creatures moving away.

Olive cannot move. She is stranded against the gate by her

own weight. Kropotkin lies flat with his nose under the gap at the bottom of the gate, snuffling and straining for a chase. Olive needs Arthur. What has happened to Arthur? What have they done to him?

And then the back door opens. 'Ollie? All right, me duck?' he calls.

'Artie,' she croaks. 'I'm here.'

He comes outside, jerky in his carpet slippers. 'What are you doing there, you daft ha'p'orth?' He holds his arm out to her. 'Get out of road, Potkins, old fella. Look what young hooligans did!' His pullover is covered in white stuff. 'Shaving foam,' he says and brushes it off.

'Whatever is happening, Artie?' Olive says.

'Just kids,' he says, 'just kids playing havoc. It's Hallowe'en, Ollie. It were kids from next door I think. Recognised little fat un. Now then, you come in and I'll make you your tea.'

'Lock Potkins up safe, won't you Artie?' she says. 'We don't want him frightened.'

Arthur urges Potkins back into his basket. 'All right, all right,' he murmurs, rubbing Kropotkin's long curly ears. 'Good dog.'

Arthur and Olive go back inside. Arthur remains in the kitchen filling the kettle and making toast. Olive returns to the front room. She stands huge in the window, her hands on her hips, her legs planted wide apart, intimidating anyone who dares to glance inside the lighted room as they pass. *Evil is abroad* are words that play in her mind, and whether it is really devils, or whether it is only kids with shaving foam and fancy dress, it makes very little difference.

'Be sure and lock that door, Artie,' she calls, and struggles back to the floor.

* * *

'Forewarned is forearmed,' says Nell to Jim. Nell listens to local radio and she knows all about Hallowe'en, all about the yobs who come round and kick old women's teeth in if they don't get their fiver. She sits in her bedroom on an upright chair, the same chair she sat in, not a year ago, watching herself become a widow in the dressing-table mirror, beside the deathbed of the stoical Jim. Her knees are locked together and her ears are on stalks.

She has switched off the downstairs lights and locked the doors and windows and sealed the letterbox with Sellotape. Upstairs the curtains are thick, and she risks a little lamp. She has the *Daily Mail* crossword on her knee and a pencil between her fingers but she cannot concentrate.

'What if Rodney knocks?' niggles Jim.

'He won't, not tonight.'

'But if he does, Nell? You can't leave our son locked out in the dark.'

'He's a grown man.'

'Still our son.'

'A grown man.'

'Nell!'

But Nell has done the thing she only does when pressed. The thing she could never do to Jim when he was a flesh-and-blood man and not just a 4″ × 3″ photograph in a frame: she flips him over onto his front to shut him up.

'Sorry, love,' she says and touches the back of the frame with her fingertips, 'but I'm anxious enough tonight without you wittering on.'

Widowhood suits Nell down to the ground. She has her pension and her house to clean and then there is Rodney who has returned, lately, to her life and who comes and goes. She's lived in this terrace all her married life – fifty years – and the neighbourhood has changed for the worst, and society has changed for the worst, but at least she has her home. At least she has her faculties.

And someone is banging on the door. Nell sits bolt-upright, listening. It's as bad as Christmas, hiding from the carol singers. Nobody could expect an old lady to open the door to strangers – but what if they break the window? There is another knock. What if it is Rodney? Perhaps it was better when he was safely locked away. She hears a faint, odd sound, like a cat. No. It is not a cat. It is somebody pretending to be a cat. This is it then. These are the trick-or-treaters. She sits cold and still as stone. She does not breathe. In her mind are towering youths in black leather and chains and they brandish flaming torches and cudgels. There is one more knock, and then silence.

She waits, straining her ears for sound of them round the back. But no. It is quiet. They have gone. She is able to breathe now, and she stands up, walks around in order to get her circulation going. Later, she decides, she'll risk creeping downstairs for a cup of tea.

This morning she spoke for the first time to the new woman next door. She has three children and is bulging with a fourth. There is a husband, or a man anyway – they just don't bother these days – but Nell has only glimpsed him once. The alleycat sort, no doubt, the sort that prowls. And she looks no better than she ought to. The sluttish type, the type that doesn't know when to stop. Like someone else. Nell purses her lips. She stands Jim up. 'A shady past,' she whispers. 'You're lucky you went when you did. You never could have stood it, the things that go on in this street nowadays.'

Jim will not answer. He is sulking.

'And where she puts all those children I don't know.' Nell laughs, catches sight of her face in the mirror, gaunt and gay. 'I saw that Olive the other day, Jim, through the window. Stands there bold as brass: light on, curtains open. Oh but she's fat,

Jim, senile I shouldn't wonder. And that Arthur! He's out at all hours with that mangy dog. Oh he's saddled good and proper now, principles or no principles.'

'He only did what he believed to be right,' sighs Jim.

'But neglecting king and country, Jim, skulking on some muddy farm while you were defending our country!'

'It was a long time ago. Shouldn't you make your peace?' Jim's voice is tentative. Behind him the sky is blue. The snap was taken before his short illness, one day when she went to the allotment with him and took a picnic lunch. It had been a beautiful summer day, his birthday. They'd had cold meat-and-potato pie, and tomatoes still warm from the sun, and a flask of tea, and he'd said it was grand. He was the photographer really. There are albums and albums of his pictures downstairs. But she took the camera from him on that occasion and snapped him, on his birthday, in his element. The corner of the shed is in the picture. Happy days. Jim was never more content than on allotment days. He might have been an educated man, he might have spent his days in the dry and papery bank, but he loved the soil. He dug and raked and sowed and hoed and passed the time of day with other gardeners, or else he sat in his shed on a canvas chair and puffed at his pipe.

'I've never had any really good veg since you went, Jim,' says Nell suddenly, with unusual sentimentality. 'But I'm sure your lovely plot will have gone to the dogs now, like everything else.'

*　*　*

'No,' says Wolfe, clutching Buffy's arm. 'Not here. We mustn't here.'

'Don't be stupid,' says Buffy. 'Get off.'

'If you're scared,' Bobby says, 'then go home to Mum.'

Wolfe knows better than to persist. He doesn't know why he wanted to come now. It sounded fun, trick-or-treating, and Buffy and Bobby thought they'd get lots of money and lots of sweets. But it is horrible. Some people won't open the door. Some people get angry and send them away. And it is scary too, in the dark street. And in his cat costume, Wolfe is cold.

'How much have you got?' asks Bobby.

'Only 50p,' Buffy says. 'Richard Barnes said he got five quid last year, and loads of chocolate.'

'Bleeding liar,' Bobby mutters.

Wolfe has only got a packet of crisps. This is a big house a long way from the road. It has rows of windows, dark and empty, but there is a light on in the hall. It feels dangerous to Wolfe, away from the lighted road between the trees.

'Don't,' he begs as Buffy lifts the heavy knocker.

'Oh shut up,' Buffy says, and the knocking echoes in the house. It is all quiet and Wolfe begins to feel relieved, and then there is the sound of a door opening deep in the house, and the sound of shuffling footsteps.

'Miaow then!' hisses Buffy.

'Miaow,' he says half-heartedly. He is fed up with being a cat. He wants to be a boy again.

The door opens. A man is there, a tall sickly man in a dressing-gown and slippers. He stands against the light so that they cannot see his face, just the tatty halo of his hair. When he speaks, his voice is old and greasy. 'Well,' he says slowly, 'what have we here?'

'Trickortreat,' say Bobby and Buffy. Buffy kicks Wolfe's ankle.

'Miaow!' he cries.

'Delightful,' the man says, rubbing his hands together. 'Trick or treat, now what shall it be?'

'Trickortreat,' they all repeat together.

'Would you like to come inside?' says the man, 'and we'll see what we can find?'

'No thanks,' says Buffy, reaching for Wolfe's hand. 'It doesn't matter. Sorry to have disturbed you.' They start to back away.

'Oh shame,' calls the man after them. 'Won't you reconsider? I've got such a lovely treat for you ∴ .' They turn away, but not before he has flicked his dressing-gown aside.

'Dirty old bugger!' shouts Bobby. 'Pervert!' And they pelt away, laughing fearfully. They run all the way to their own street, Buffy dragging Wolfe who keeps on treading on his tail.

'Told you we shouldn't . . .' pants Wolfe eventually, when they've stopped and are leaning against their own front wall, catching their breath.

'Shut your face,' says Bobby.

'I've lost my crisps!' wails Wolfe.

'Shall we tell Mum about the man?' asks Buffy.

'No,' Bobby says, 'She'd only worry. She'd probably call the police or something stupid. That would be *really* embarrassing.'

'We'd better go down the chippie then,' says Buffy. 'My lantern's gone out, has yours? I'm leaving it here.' They all leave their pumpkins on the wall and trail off dispiritedly down the hill to the chip shop. Wolfe's tights sag at the back so that a little semicircle of bottom shows above the droop of his tail.

*   *   *

'Oh, switch it off,' says Olive. It is a load of rubbish these days, a load of drivel. Arthur switches off the television and the room is loud with silence. 'That's better,' Olive says. 'Can't bear it sometimes, Artie, the way it goes on and on, one thing after another, no time to think. Is it my age, Artie? Or is it my nerves?'

Arthur bends over and brushes her hair with his lips. 'It's discrimination,' he decides. 'You're a discriminating woman. You're the lass I met fifty-odd years back. A lass with a mind of her own.'

Olive snorts. 'A mind of my own. Don't know about that. Don't know what's up with me, lately. Getting dull. Can't string two thoughts together any more. And I never was stupid, was I?'

'You never were. Maybe you're tired.'

'But I never do anything! What shall I do? What did I ever do?'

'Come on, now . . .'

'Remember the games, Artie, how we used to play games? Silly games, word games?'

'Aye, I remember. What were that daft one? Word associations or somat.'

'That's it! Let's play. Let me see if I can still play.'

Arthur hesitates. 'I don't know . . .'

'Oh go on Artie, you start.' Olive looks expectantly at him and he grins.

'Oh all right. Er . . . let me think. Earth.'

'Sun.'

'Sky.'

'That's it!'

'Go on then. Sky.'

'Cloud.'

'Good. Rain.'

'Spain.'

Arthur looks perplexed.

'You know, Artie. What is it? The rain in Spain rains mainly on the –'

'Plain.'

'Plane. Er . . . sky.'

'Had it.'

'Have we, Artie? All right. Tree?'

'Green.'

'Leaves.'

'Cabbage.'

'Food.'

'Drink.' Olive's eyes slide vaguely away.

'Good,' says Arthur. 'See, you can do it. You can still play.'

'Drink,' insists Olive. 'Go on Artie, pour me a drink.'

'You know what the doctor said.'

'Oh bugger the doctor.'

'All right. Just a drop then.' Arthur is incapable of denying Olive anything. He takes two misty gold-ringed glasses from the cupboard and pours a drop of brandy into each.

'I *was* beautiful once, wasn't I Artie? In those days I was,' Olive pleads suddenly. She fills the floor in front of the gas fire. Her colourless hair is an orange cloud, stained by its glow. One of her cheeks is baked pink in its heat. Her breasts are massive under her woollen jumper. On her feet are big man's slippers and baggy socks.

'You were, me duck.'

'More beautiful than *her*.'

'Who?'

'The new woman next door. I saw you looking, Artie. The one with all the children.'

'Olive! And you *were* beautiful.'

'I had my chances, you know. Could've had anyone. *Anyone*. My waist was twenty-two inches, you know, Arthur, and the men used to look at me. They all wanted me, like that, they all wanted me. I used to tease them, you know Artie, on the ward.'

'I bet they didn't know what'd hit them, a nurse like you!'

'But I was a good nurse. I'd give them the eye though . . . speed up recovery, or just cheer the poor buggers up. I could've had any one of them.'

'I know that, Ollie. I know how lucky I was.'

Olive swallows her brandy and subsides. Arthur fetches her tin of sweets. 'Here we are,' he says, and places them beside her on the floor. The room fills with the crackling of paper and the sound of her chewing and sucking the sticky caramels against her teeth.

She drifts back to the years before the war. Amongst those years are days that are as glossy in her memory as the photographs in an expensive book. Half her time then was taken up with work and the rest with cycling across the city to attend meetings, so that there was hardly the time left to sleep. Those were the days when sleep seemed a nuisance, a waste of crucial time, for that was the time before the danger of Hitler was widely realised, when Arthur and his kind laboured to make people wake up to the threat of another world war. Those were the days when she was the most alive, when she was the most engaged with the world: the days of her life that mattered.

'Allotment tomorrow if weather's right,' Arthur says. 'Might get broad beans in. Might lift first parsnips. Best if they're frosted but we could have some with our Sunday dinner.'

'And what will I do?' asks Olive in a caramel splutter.

'You can rest, Ollie, or go for walk. Doctor said you should make effort. Get out in air.'

'Maybe I'll take Potty,' Olive says. 'Yes, I will. I'll wear my cherry hat and I'll take Potkins for a walk.'

*   *   *

The house is warm when the children get back and they sit at the kitchen table eating their chips with greasy fingers. Petra leans over Bobby's shoulder and takes one. 'Mum!' he complains.

Petra's face is white. Wolfe holds out his biggest chip to her. She looks tired and fat with the new baby stretching her jumper out of shape.

'Well?' she says. 'Tell me how you got on. Was it good? Did you have fun? Did anyone actually give you anything?'

'It was all right,' says Buffy with her mouth full.

Petra takes Wolfe's chip and smiles at him. 'Did you get anything Wolfie?' Wolfe shakes his head. 'What's the matter?' She can always tell. She can see inside him and always tell when he is sad. 'It was all right, wasn't it? No one was horrible to you? Oh I *knew* I shouldn't have let you go.'

'It was all right,' says Bobby. Buffy looks warningly at Wolfe, but he won't say anything anyway. He tries not to say things to Petra that will worry her more.

'It was all right, Mum,' he says. Poor Petra. She was all right when they were at the Longhouse. They were quite happy then, all of them. Wolfe aches with homesickness when he remembers the warm crowdedness of it and he thinks that Petra does too. They were all settled until she had to go and fall in love with Tom and start another baby, and move them all up North to be with him. But Tom hasn't been around much lately, and Petra has always got red eyes and she is always sniffling.

In the Longhouse there was always someone to talk to when you were worried, but here there is no one.

'It will be good living in a little house,' Petra had told them. 'Just think, our own kitchen, our own decisions – no more meetings! No more rotas!' But even then, even before they left, Wolfe thought that her voice sounded wavery, as if she wasn't really sure.

At first it *had* been fun. Wolfe loves his own room where he can shut the door and no one steals his socks or borrows his books without asking him. But that is the only thing that is better. He misses the huge garden and the chickens and the big black stove where you can dry your gloves and warm your bum. He misses his friends. And when the baby comes, when it is big enough to sleep away from Petra it will sleep with him. So it won't be just his room any more.

Petra doesn't look like the other children's mothers at Wolfe's new school. She wears the wrong sort of clothes. She looks older than them, and she looks younger. She looks younger because she doesn't wear lipstick or stuff round her eyes, and she doesn't wear high heels to make her walk like a mother; and she looks older because she looks so sad. There are grooves ready for tears on her cheeks, and very long grey bits in her trailing hair.

Wolfe misses his friends at the Longhouse. They never made fun of his name. Nobody likes Wolfe at his new school because he talks funny, but that is all right because he doesn't like them either. They think he's scruffy and his hair is too long. And they look at his skin in a funny way. And in country dancing nobody will hold his hand because of his eczema. *And* they make fun of his name.

'You can finish my chips, I'm full,' he says to Petra.

'Lovely,' says Petra, 'I'm quite hungry now.' She squeezes herself onto the edge of his chair.

'Why did you have to go and call me Wolfe?' he asks suddenly. Petra looks at him, surprised.

'Because you're so ugly,' Buffy says, pulling a face at him. '*We* got named after singers, Bobby and me, didn't we Mum? Because we're stars.'

Petra ignores her. 'When you were born you were covered in long hairs,' she explains. Wolfe grimaces. 'And it was very strange because just before you were born I'd had an amazing dream about a wolf, a very kind and wise wolf that walked about on two legs like a man. I didn't mean to call you Wolfe, it just sort of happened. I was going to call you that until I thought of something else ... and it just stuck. Anyway, I think it's quite distinguished. It suits you.'

'It's a bit embarrassing for him,' says Buffy.

'No it's not,' says Petra.

'It is, isn't it?' Buffy arches her eyebrows at Wolfe.

'Sort of,' he agrees. 'I do like it, Mum, honest. It's just that the kids here tease me about it.'

'Oh dear.' Petra presses her lips together until they go white at the edges, and the dark wriggly lines that Wolfe hates appear on her forehead.

'But it doesn't matter,' he insists. 'Don't worry.'

'Well,' Petra sighs and gets up and collects together the greasy chip papers. She screws them into a big ball. 'I'm afraid if they want to tease you they'll find something. If it's not your name it's your teeth or your ears, or something.'

'Or my skin,' Wolfe whispers.

'Where's Tom?' asks Bobby suddenly.

'Out,' Petra says in her quick voice, the voice that means No more questions. But from the way Bobby and Buffy exchange glances it is clear that they have planned this. Planned to find out what's happening.

'Out where?' Buffy dares. 'He's always out.'

'I haven't even seen him for days,' adds Bobby.

'You haven't split up, have you?'

Petra throws the paper in the bin and the lid snaps down sharply. 'Of course not,' she says, but she does not turn round to look at them. Wolfe can see from the way her back is scrunched up that they might have done. That Petra is not sure. 'I want all that black plastic and all those pumpkin seeds cleared up from the front-room carpet before you go to bed,' she says, and she sounds as if she might be going to cry again and Wolfe is cross with Bobby and Buffy. And cross with Tom.

He sits on his hands to stop himself scratching, pressing them with his legs against the hard chair-edge until they hurt, because the pain is more bearable than the itching. His skin has been worse since they've been here. It is always worse when he's unhappy. The backs of his knees and his hands are worst. First the blisters come, terribly itchy like little tight seed-pearls, and he has to watch himself all the time to stop scratching, but even if he manages all day he will scratch at night and wake up to find himself bleeding where his nails have raked his skin. Bobby and Buffy won't have his sheets on their beds because of the blood-stains all over them. Poor Petra has tried everything. First he couldn't have milk or eggs, then everything had to be washed in special stuff, and he's had so many different creams to rub on and none of them very much good . . . He tries to hide it from Petra mostly because it makes her so unhappy. It makes her worry. And so he tries not to make a fuss. But it is like a terrible burning, a terrible, teasing, itching burn. And it is ugly. It makes him ugly. No wonder nobody likes him here, with his ugly skin and his stupid name.

* * *

Olive is dozing on the floor now. She always dozes in the evenings, and Arthur chances switching the television back on with the volume turned right down. There is a comedy on about some people who are divorced and their stepchildren. He chuckles obediently along with the studio audience, and is sorry when it's finished. Evenings are long now that the clocks have gone back. He gets restless in the evenings, always restless with nothing much to do.

At the allotment it will be quiet now, silent, except for the rushing over stones of the dark river below. The earth will be soft and moist on this mild night, fine clean earth, earth that Arthur has created over fifty years. The turnips and the parsnips are huddled in the ground, their pale shoulders just showing above the blanket of the earth. Tomorrow he'll ease some of them up, the fat and tapering bodies, cloaked in his earth. And it's all there, waiting for him. In two days' time the moon will be full and that means it is the time to sow seeds. He might get in a first sowing of broad beans, even peas perhaps for an early crop. He rubs his hands together pleasurably. That's the beauty of working on the allotment – there's always something to do, something to draw you through the seasons, through the years.

Olive snorts and jerks. Her teeth have slipped. He helps her sit up. 'All right, me duck?' he asks.

'It's these blessed caramels,' she replies, sleepily.

'Let's get you upstairs then.'

Arthur helps her to her feet and then to the bottom of the stairs. 'You get yourself up and ready and I'll bring up your cocoa in a bit,' Arthur says. He watches her climbing the stairs, slowly, pausing on each step for a moment with both feet, and panting with the effort. The seat of her skirt is stretched out of shape by her huge backside. A memory flickers just for a moment, the image of her young bottom bobbing up the stairs. Oh she used to run about starkers, and he loved to see her – big, soft breasts and all the rest of her muscular, tight and rippling, buttocks round as stones. Now she blots out the light with her hugeness.

Half-way up she stops. 'Arthur!' she calls, and looks down at him. 'Arthur, you never got me any tea tonight.'

'I did, Ollie. We had toasted cheese. We had a nice bit of toasted cheese and an Eccles cake.'

'Oh . . . oh did we?' Olive continues her climb. Arthur watches her bulky back for a moment more, shaking his head, and then he goes out to give Kropotkin a last turn around the block. It will be half an hour before she's ready for her cocoa.

Two

Olive hollows the mattress in a great snoring scoop and Arthur has to strain not to be engulfed. A grey wash illuminates the room and all its contents. He lies for a moment looking at the scraps of their lives pinned upon the walls and arranged on the mantelpiece of the old cast-iron fireplace, and on the window-sill. There are pamphlets, and newspaper cuttings, reports of an anti-Fascist rally that they had helped to organise. That was what brought them together, the common enemy. They had marched before the danger was widely realised, they had marched full of determination, and in the curling clippings they march still. In one of the photographs, the young Olive, faded now but still vital, waves her arm angrily. Her hair is flying out and her mouth is open in a shout. She had such red lips then, such black black hair. Beside her there is her mother's splashy painting of Mount Etna erupting. And there are fiddly things – presents, china bits of this and that, artificial flowers, things she never really cared about, things he's been the one to dust over the years.

Mount Etna glows now as the light catches the glass and Arthur clambers up out of Olive's warmth and out of bed. He sleeps in old yellowish long johns and a long-sleeved vest and, shivering, he piles his other clothes on top. He wears his favourite trousers since he's off to the allotment – dark brown corduroy, furrowed like the earth. He puts his hand into the pocket and feels the godstone there. It is a white glassy pebble, smooth and faintly warm to the touch. The stone has been his for well-nigh fifty years. He remembers the first time he held it in his palm, warm and precious as an egg, comforting, fitting the hollow of his hand as if it had been moulded there. 'That's a precious stone,' his mate, Bill, had said. 'Not money-precious, nothing so common as that.' Bill is dead now, long, long dead. But the stone is warm in Arthur's hand. 'That must be passed on,' Bill had said, 'and I think you're the one to have it. To keep it safe, until you're done with it.' They had been standing together on the dense fertile earth with the first tips of green all around them, and the sky a flapping sheet, and the wind had blown tears into Bill's eyes before he turned away. With the stone, Bill passed on to Arthur the beginnings of his great knowledge. He taught him to test the temperature of the soil with his skin, to judge the character of the seasons, to watch the phases of the moon and to work within her rhythms. Arthur has treasured the godstone ever since that day and, whether it has any influence or not, everything Arthur plants grows as if charmed. Arthur has green fingers, he has the secrets Bill taught him, and the wisdom of half a century of working with the soil, and even without the godstone his plants would be bound to flourish – but the godstone is Arthur's talisman and now he holds it in his hand for just a moment as he watches the rising, falling form of Olive beneath the bedclothes. He finishes dressing, scoops Chairman Mao from the bed, carries him downstairs and puts him outside. Kropotkin yaps excitedly from the outhouse and Arthur lets him out, old grizzled dog, wagging and smiling and panting with joy.

'Good dog, good old lad,' Arthur rubs the curls of his neck and the animal groans with pleasure. Chairman Mao, shivering, slinks under a bush where he does his business and arrives back at the door, blue and mottled already although it is not an especially cold morning.

Arthur breathes deeply. 'It's a grand day,' he declares. 'I'll get off early and make the best of it.' The sky is pearly pale, innocent, but Arthur is aware that the ripple of cloud in the west might well mean rain.

He takes a cup of tea upstairs to Olive. 'Morning me duck,' he says. He shakes her shoulder until her snoring shudders and stops and she opens her eyes a fraction. They are bright slits like the eyes of a little girl peeping through a mask. 'All right now?' he asks, and helps her up, props her with her back against the pillows. She frowns at him. She's never been any good in the mornings, not till she's had her cup of tea and time to separate herself from the unfathomable depths of her sleep. She goes so much deeper than Arthur, who hovers and flickers all night on the line between asleep and awake. He envies Olive her ability to plummet straight through.

Olive fumbles for her teeth and Arthur passes them to her. She puts them in and clamps her jaws until they sit comfortably. They are sticky still, and sweet with the caramel that is jammed in their crevices.

'Morning,' she croaks, and takes the cup of tea.

'I thought, Ollie, if it's all right with you, I'd get straight off. Looks like rain. I'll be back soon after dinner.' Olive grunts. 'There's ham in the fridge for your dinner, you can do yourself a sandwich then I'll do you chips for your tea. Chips and egg, eh?' Olive sips her tea. 'I'll put your clothes out for you here, and I'll fetch your hat down. Potkins is looking forward to his walk.'

'If you say so. Where's Mao?'

'He's downstairs, Ollie. He's been out so he'll be all right till I get back.' Arthur arranges Olive's clothes on the end of the bed. 'All right, then? Need the lav before I go?' Olive shakes her head. He kisses her, and creaks off downstairs. Olive listens to him whistling. Already his mind is on the allotment, messing with the soil. He doesn't get up there so much now, but still he loves it. Loves it more than anything. More than anything except Olive. She finishes her tea and slides luxuriously back down into the bed. Mao materialises on the pillow beside her just as she hears the door bang downstairs.

With a pitiful little cry, a new-baby cry, he snuggles his cold smooth body down inside her nightdress, and curls himself up, vibrating with pleasure, against the warmth of her breasts.

*   *   *

'Hello Mum.' Rodney comes in through the back door looking taller and more disreputable than ever. 'How are you?' He hugs her so that her face is squashed against the roughness of his donkey jacket.

'Oh Rodney!' Nell pulls away from him, pleased and cross, rearranging her hair with her fingers. 'I expect you're after a cup of tea? Well that's *all* you'll get this morning. I'm all upside-down. Won't get to shops till after dinner if I stop now.' She fills the kettle.

Rodney sits down at the table, starts flicking through the *Mail*.

'Well take your coat off, our Rodney, if you're staying for a bit,' Nell says. Rodney is her pleasure and her shame. He is her own, her only flesh and blood and he isn't a bad son. Since he's been free he's been coming to see her three or four times a week. He's a good boy like that, not neglectful. And now that Jim has passed on she gets lonely. He is a dutiful boy. But he is not a boy. Perhaps it would be all right if he was, but he is nearing fifty and his hair is grey and thinning on top, and he has no job and never even seems to look. He lives in a hostel, a place for people like him who have been inside. Nell visited once, but only once. She found it a sordid, peeling place. She hardly liked to breathe the stale old-smoky air while she was there, let alone touch anything or sit on the greasy chair that was offered in the reception room. No, far better she stay away and Rodney visit her here where at least it is clean. Fancy Nell having a criminal for a son! She can never get used to the idea. But then that is all behind him now, touch wood. She presses her fingers fervently against the Formica front of the cutlery drawer. It is shameful to have a son with badness in him, and Nell has no illusions about him, no secret hope that none of it was true. She knows he was bad and simply hopes that he has learnt his lesson, that he is bad no more. And anyway, Rodney is God's will, she thinks, puzzled and resigned, putting his cup of tea down in front of him.

'You didn't call round last night?' she asks. 'Only I wouldn't have answered.'

'Oh, what were you up to?'

'Nothing. I locked the door against . . . against Hallowe'en. You get all sorts round these days, knocking, begging, so I locked the door. Better safe than sorry I say, only it did occur to me that you might have called.'

'No. He stayed put last night. Skint. Watched a film on the box, about an ice skater.'

Nell wipes her hands on her apron and sits down opposite him. It annoys her the way he does that, always an alibi on the tip of his tongue, slick as you like.

'You don't have to explain yourself to me, our Rodney. A grown man.'

Rodney slurps his tea. 'Anything want doing now he's here?'

'You can take the bins round the front, save the binmen coming down the passage in their filthy boots. What are you doing later?'

'He's going up the post office to cash his giro and then he's off to town. He'll read the papers in the library. He'll have a pint for his dinner.'

Nell shakes her head. It seems such a terrible waste. He spends all his days like that since he's been out: sitting in the reference library reading the papers; sitting in the pub; sitting in her kitchen drinking tea; sitting anywhere where he can soak up a bit of warmth for free. And he was such a bright lad, such an adorable boy. Now his face is dull and whiskery. His eyes, once so big and blue that women cooed into his pram and swore he'd be a stealer of hearts, are bloodshot now and shifty, hidden behind the thick and smeary lenses of his black-rimmed spectacles. He has a sour, unhealthy smell. He makes her kitchen reek of his filthy hostel. Hard to remember the milky sweetness of his baby self, and how she used to bury her nose in the soft skin at the back of his neck when he was warm and fragrant from his bath.

'Well it's all right for some,' she says. 'I only wish I had time to sit around pleasing myself. Some of us have more . . . more purpose.'

'Don't get your knickers in a twist,' Rodney says. 'He could do with a top-up.'

Nell tips a fierce stream of tea into his cup. 'However you manage on your own, I don't know,' she grumbles.

'Funny you should say that,' he grins at her through scummy teeth, 'only it's getting near time he moved out of the hostel. It's only temporary accommodation, you know, just till he gets himself back on his feet.'

'And you haven't shown much sign of that, have you? Oh no, I've bailed you out often enough. I'm not as soft as your poor father, God bless his soul.'

'Not money, you old bag.'

'Rodney!'

'He wants to move back here.'

Nell frowns. 'What do you mean?'

'He means what he says. He wants to move back home. Wouldn't you like that?'

'No I b— well wouldn't!'

'Mum . . .'

'I've got my own life to live now, Rodney. Independence.'

'Well he doesn't know what he'll do then.' Rodney looks nonplussed. His big bad man's hands lie limp upon her nice clean table. He looks pleadingly at Nell and she gets up, wipes her hands on her apron, busies herself. 'He'll get off then,' he says. His voice is flat. He is upset. He goes. She hears the clatter and clank of him moving the bins and then his heavy footsteps thudding away. Her heart is heavy. He is her son, when all's said and done. She wipes the table, very thoroughly, with a J Cloth. There is a drop of tea. There are the invisible prints of his none-too-clean hands.

She rinses the cloth and stands at the sink, gazing sightlessly out of the window. She thinks about Miles, her brother Edwin's son. Miles is an architect with a wife and two children of his own. He is a credit to Edwin, a credit to the whole family. The thought of him sticks like a burr in Nell's throat. She hasn't seen him for years, not Miles, not even Edwin. Last time the families had been together it had been Christmas. Nell gazes at her tiny distorted reflection in the gleaming tap as it comes back to her. It had been an awkward occasion. Jim and Edwin had put on a good show, filling the house with cigar smoke and toasting the Queen, but Daphne, Edwin's wife, and Nell had never hit it off. During a cold Boxing Day tea of wet lettuce and sliced tongue, Rodney had disgraced himself at the table. Quite suddenly, in the middle of a polite silence, he'd said, 'Buggeration,' belched resoundingly and slithered down under the table. Edwin and Jim had hauled him out and Edwin had pronounced him dead drunk, and Nell had caught the smirk on Daphne's face, and no, Nell couldn't see the funny side, and that was that, Christmas over, the feeble attempt at a festive spirit quenched.

And that was the last they'd seen of Edwin's family. Rodney had left home shortly after that, and then there was the disgrace, and Nell could never stand the thought of the condescension, the pity, the smugness of Daphne and the perfect, polite and brainy Miles, and so she'd rejected Edwin's attempts to help. For what help *was* there? All that is left now between Nell and her brother are Christmas cards:

perishing glitter-encrusted landscapes with muffled coachmen and frozen lakes.

Nell sighs, almost regretfully, and then she goes upstairs to Jim.

* * *

Tom is sitting at the kitchen table. He is rolling a cigarette. Wolfe watches the way he conjures the strings of brown tobacco into a neat white paper sausage, puts it in his mouth and, squinting down at it, flicks it alight with his lighter.

'Hello, mate,' Tom says, when he's breathed out his first mouthful of smoke. He stretches out his arm and Wolfe allows himself to be drawn close.

'Where've you been?' Wolfe asks. Tom smells of tobacco and hair and other grown-up things.

'Out and about, mate. Missed me?'

'Don't know. Mum has,' Wolfe says. 'I thought you'd gone and left us.'

'Hmmm,' Tom puffs on his cigarette. He has sleep in the corners of his eyes, and a crumpled-sheet print on his cheek, and stubble on his chin like that on the iron-filings man Wolfe got in his stocking at Christmas. There are shiny red hollows on either side of his nose where his glasses usually sit.

'Are you staying then?' Wolfe persists. 'Did you sleep with my mum last night?' Tom does not answer immediately, and will not meet Wolfe's eyes, and Wolfe pulls away from him. 'Did you?'

'I slept here last night,' Tom says.

'Are you still living here then?'

'Hold on a minute,' Tom says. 'I don't know. Neither of us knows. OK? How are you anyway? How's school?'

'Terrible.' Wolfe finds a clean dish and fills it with three

Weetabix and a heap of brown sugar. He gets himself a spoon, splashes in milk, and stands at the end of the table eating.

Tom watches him. 'No school today?'

'Half-term.'

'Ah . . .' Tom grinds out his cigarette on a saucer, gets up and puts the kettle on. 'It's the 1st of November,' he says. 'Christ, how the time passes.'

'A pinch and a punch for the first of the month,' says Wolfe gloomily.

'Cheer up, old mate.' Tom turns and ruffles Wolfe's hair. 'Tell you what, have you got anything fixed for Bonfire Night?'

'Nope.'

'I'll come round then, shall I, and bring a box of fireworks? And could you and Buffy and Bobby get a bonfire together? Could you do that?'

'Yes,' says Wolfe solemnly. 'I expect so. But if you're *coming round* on Bonfire Night, that means you won't *be* here already. That means you *don't* live here any more.'

'Clever little bugger aren't you?' Tom says, grinning and picking a shred of tobacco from between his teeth. 'I told you. I don't know. It's all in a state of flux.'

'What's that?'

'Change. In other words I'm not sure. Not right now. Your mum and I need a bit of space.'

'Oh yes,' Wolfe nods, wisely. People were always saying that at the Longhouse, that they needed space. 'Flux,' Wolfe says. It is a good word. 'Flux.' There was always a state of flux at the Longhouse, always people coming and going.

'Mum's been crying,' says Wolfe.

'Oh Christ.' Tom picks up his glasses from the table, rubs them on his shirt and puts them on.

'What about the baby?'

Tom doesn't answer. He pours boiling water into the tea-pot and stirs the teabags round with a spoon. He doesn't let it brew, not like Petra. He doesn't even put the lid on, let alone the tea-cosy. 'I'm taking her up some tea,' Tom says, pouring it into a mug.

'It'll be too weak,' Wolfe says, 'she doesn't like it weak. She calls it gnat's piss.'

Tom shrugs. 'Think about the bonfire, won't you?'

'All right.'

'By the way, you haven't seen my shaving foam have you?' Tom asks.

'No,' Wolfe says. He waits till Tom's gone upstairs, then he brushes the shreds of tobacco off the table and sits down to read about Desperate Dan in his comic. And as he reads, he scratches.

*   *   *

Olive wakes because her bladder is full. She lifts Chairman Mao away from her and begins the long heave out of bed. It takes her a good few minutes of grunting and huffing and puffing before she manages to swing her legs over the edge. She sits for a moment on the edge, shivering in her nylon nightgown, before lowering her feet to the cold lino floor. It is old brown-and-orange-patterned lino, worn through in places to its stringy backing. They never bothered much about homey things, Olive and Arthur, when they were young. They were always looking outwards at the world. Home was merely a place to eat and sleep, to catch their breath, and so they never got round to carpets in the bedrooms, and now they never will. There is a small rag rug, and Olive stands on it while she pulls her candlewick dressing-gown around her. Mao hunches in the warm place she's left, regarding her balefully.

'Can't stay in bed all day,' she says, and he yawns and turns his back on her. Clearly, he doesn't agree.

She goes to the bathroom and notices that the house is very quiet. 'Artie . . .' she calls, but her voice hangs cold in the air.

It takes her a long time to dress. Her clothes wait for her in an ordered pile, underwear on top. Everything is clean and ironed, for Arthur likes things immaculate. It used to drive Olive mad, slapdash Olive, when they were young. Finicky, she used to call him, pernickety, but now she can see the sense. She appreciates the order he imposes, for the rest of the world makes no sense at all.

'Arthur!' she calls again, and again there is no reply. He must have gone out. Inconsiderate. Not like Arthur. Age creeping up. Olive struggles into her vest, a thermal vest, a present from Arthur last Christmas. She pauses, remembering the time of year. Is Christmas approaching again already? Or has it passed? Alone in the house her memory crumples and she cannot read the date. 'Artie!' But all is quiet. Her feet are cold and she bends painfully and puts on some socks. They share socks, Olive and Arthur, for they are easier and warmer for Olive than stockings. Suspenders! How she used to hate suspenders with those fiddly clips, soft, pink, rubbery to slide into place, and how Arthur loved them, unclipping them, just the thing for Arthur, neat and tidy. But then he didn't have to wear them. She pulls on her frock and her cardigan and then she sees her hat. It is a black straw hat with a bunch of scarlet wax cherries on the brim, and a cherry-coloured ribbon. 'Arthur?' she calls again, puzzled, but then the fog clears and she catches a glimpse of the day ahead. 'Of course, Mao!' she exclaims. 'Artie's up on his bloody allotment, and I must take Potkins for a walk.'

Downstairs the clock tells her that it is already half-past ten, and the calendar that it is 1st November. That is good. She knows where she is, then. It is a bright day, the sun floods the kitchen. Arthur has left everything ready: teapot empty with the teabags beside it, bread and lime marmalade cut into triangles, a cup and saucer with the milk already in. Olive switches on the kettle and goes out to greet Kropotkin.

He bounds from the outhouse, delirious with pleasure, and Olive rubs his curly head. Above his grunts and snuffles she can hear voices in next-door's garden. The new neighbours. They may have been there weeks. Months? But she's never spoken to them. There's a woman and several noisy children. She goes to the wall and peers over.

'Morning,' she says, and the woman looks up and smiles.

'Pleased to meet you.' She is a short woman with an enormous pregnant belly. Beside her stands a small stout boy. 'I'm Petra,' she continues, 'and this is Wolfe.'

'Wolfe?' repeats Olive. 'That's a fancy name. Is it the fashion?'

Petra laughs. 'No, I'm afraid not.' The small boy scowls. 'I met your husband the other day, he was telling me about his allotment.'

'Husband?' says Olive. 'No.'

'Oh . . . your brother?'

'No.'

'Oh well, sorry . . . I just assumed . . .'

'Mum's not married neither,' says Wolfe.

'Wolfe!'

'Well that *is* all the fashion now isn't it?' Olive says. 'Artie's my lodger, no relation.'

'Oh, I see. Well he seems very nice whoever he is.'

'He's a wonder.'

'I'm just thinking about making a start on the garden,' Petra says. 'It's such a mess, depressing, but I don't know.'

'Well I'd like to plant a tree,' Wolfe says. 'We might not live here for long. But I'd still like to plant a tree.'

Petra shrugs and smiles. She has a very white face and it is hard to tell how old she is. There are lines round her eyes but her smile is girlish. She has long hair, fair streaked with grey, tied back from her face with an Indian scarf. She is pretty, but not a patch on Olive as a lass.

'You ought to ask my Artie about that,' Olive says to Wolfe. 'He knows all about growing things.'

'Thanks,' says Petra. 'You'd like that, wouldn't you, Wolfe?' Wolfe scuffs his shoes in the dirt.

'He's up on allotment today,' Olive says. 'Same plot he's had since 1934.'

'Really! That's amazing!'

'What's an allotment?' asks Wolfe.

'A little plot of land,' explains Petra, 'like an extra garden where people grow vegetables.'

'And all sorts else,' adds Olive.

Kropotkin begins to bark and Olive looks round. There is steam billowing from the kitchen door. 'Breakfast-time,' she says. 'Kettle boiling.'

'Well, it's been nice to meet you,' Petra says.

'Nice little chap, Wolfe.' Olive looks at him wistfully for a moment, and then gropes her way into the steamy kitchen to find her breakfast.

* * *

'What a fat woman,' says Wolfe. 'Mum, why is she so fat?'

Petra winces and puts her finger to her lips: 'Shhh.'

'Anyway, I do want to grow a tree,' Wolfe says. 'And we could grow some other things too, couldn't we? Like at the Longhouse.'

'I don't know.' They look critically at the small rectangular garden. There is a patch of grass, a holly bush, a tangle of old herbs – mint and lemon balm and sage – and lots of weeds. Wolfe thinks longingly of the grounds of their last home, of the orchard with its long rough grass and friendly mossy trees, of

the big vegetable garden, of the greenhouse with its warm
tomato stink.

'We could dig up the grass and plant potatoes,' suggests
Wolfe.

'Hmmm, I don't know, love. Once you start growing things
it means you're staying put. Literally putting down roots.'

'*Are* we moving then?'

'Oh, I don't know.'

'You're in a state of flux,' says Wolfe proudly and Petra
laughs.

'That's about the size of it.'

'Tom said that, about flux.'

'Oh he did, did he? And what else did he say?'

Wolfe screws up his nose. 'Don't know. Not much. He said
he's coming round on Bonfire Night. He wants me to build him
a bonfire.'

'Oh yes, he said.' Petra picks off a withered mint leaf,
crushes it between her fingers and sniffs them.

'Can we make toffee? Bonfire toffee?'

'Yes, all right.'

'Do you want him to come round?'

'Tom? Yes, no . . . Oh I don't know.' Petra turns towards
him and bends down, her hands on his shoulders. She looks at
him almost fiercely and Wolfe swallows, alarmed. 'It will be all
right,' she says. 'We'll be all right, Tom or no Tom. You're not
to worry.'

'But what about the baby?'

Petra shrugs and stands straight again. She puts her hand in
the small of her back where the baby makes it ache.

'Well anyway, I've never had a dad and I'm all right,' says
Wolfe, stoutly.

Petra sighs, and the skin between her eyebrows furrows into
a frown. Wolfe hates it when she frowns like that, she looks
old and cross, like a witch in a book. He looks away.

'Can we move back to the Longhouse?' he asks.

'I only wish . . .' begins Petra, then, 'no, I don't think so. There was somebody else, a man with a couple of kids moving in. There won't be room for us now. Anyway, I don't like the idea of moving back, going back . . .'

'Oh.' Wolfe kicks around in the dirt and finds an old toy car, its wheels clogged with earth. 'I do,' he says.

'That's nice,' says Petra looking at the car. But she doesn't mean it, she doesn't even see it, her eyes are focused somewhere far away. She wears a flowered dress this morning and the baby inside her doesn't look so big, and she wears wellington boots that still have Longhouse earth in their treads. Wolfe thinks she looks nice. He can see the head of the old woman next door the other side bobbing up and down above the half net curtain at her kitchen windows as if she is working hard, scrubbing something perhaps. A moment later, water gushes from her kitchen drainpipe and froths in the drain, and then the door opens and she comes out carrying a bowl of steamy washing. She ignores Petra and Wolfe at first, but that is silly. It is obvious that she can see them, for there is only a low scrubby hedge between the two gardens.

'Good morning,' Petra says.

The old woman nods her head towards them, and gives a stiff smile. She is the opposite of Olive, Wolfe thinks, long and skinny with a pointed nose. She is all sharp in the places where Olive is round.

'Lovely day,' persists Petra. 'We're just thinking about tackling the garden.'

Nell sniffs. 'Nice enough so far,' she says, 'but the forecast is rain. My Rodney will do mine I expect.' She looks with satisfaction at her neatly paved garden. 'Easy to maintain,' she explains. 'My Jim did it before he . . . Just a few little spaces for bedding plants in the spring and the rest just wants a good sweep, a swill-over with bleach to kill the moss now and then.'

Wolfe sees Petra's lips twitch. 'We're planting a tree,' he says.

'Oh . . . Well only a little one I hope.'

Wolfe looks at Petra. 'I was talking to the man from next door yesterday,' she says, changing the subject. 'Olive's lodger.'

'Lodger! Is that what she calls it!'

'Oh . . .' Petra hesitates. 'Anyway, he's a keen gardener, isn't he? He was telling me all about his allotment.'

Nell comes to the fence, and leans towards them so that Wolfe can see the long powdery slits of her nostrils. 'Communists, you know, the pair of them,' she hisses. Wolfe and Petra exchange glances. She moves back and speaks in her normal voice. 'My Jim now, God bless him, *he* was the one to talk to about allotments. Best root crops in South Yorkshire. You name it, he won a show with it.'

'Is he dead?' Wolfe asks.

Nell gives him a freezing look. 'I only wish our Rodney would carry on the tradition but . . . he hasn't got the touch. I mean green fingers,' she says hastily. 'But he's a good lad. He'll keep my back tidy for me.'

'Rodney's your son?' hazards Petra. 'Any grandchildren?'

'No. Our Rodney's not what you might call a family man.' Her eyes rest on Wolfe for a moment and then twitch away. 'Well, must get on, lots to do.' She turns abruptly from Petra and Wolfe to peg her tea-towels and aprons on the line.

*　　*　　*

Nell peels off her rubber gloves. Her hands are moist and sweaty inside from the heat of the water and she rinses them under the cold tap and dries them carefully on a towel. She dries between each finger, shuddering at the thought of the scabby little boy next door. Diseased. And then she thinks of Rodney. It is time for her morning coffee. She heats milk in a pan, and as she watches the surface haze over and begin to bubble, she decides to look at the albums. Just a bit of a look at some of Jim's pictures. She hasn't looked at them for years. It was always Jim who was the one for photographs. Always framing a scene with his fingers, always snapping away, always working in the cellar in the chemical-smelling blackness to bring the pictures floating to life. He could have done it for a living if he'd had half a mind. They'd discussed it once, early on, but the bank was steadier.

She flinches, remembering a humiliation during the war, during the time Jim was home convalescing after his wound. He'd been down in the cellar one night developing some pictures, and someone passing had seen the little red light that he used through the grille over the coal-hole. Someone had seen it flashing and word went round that he was signalling to the Germans, that he was a spy! Her Jim, a traitor! Nell blamed it on Olive living so close, a Communist, or near as damn it, and Arthur a conscientious objector. Conchy my foot, she thinks, coward more like.

The albums are all there in the sideboard, all labelled with date and subject. Nell chooses an early one, bound in blue leather. She sits with her coffee beside her and turns the pages. FIRST FAMILY PICNIC, she reads, JULY 1940. There is the checked tablecloth, and there she is in her tailored suit, tailored by herself out of striped mattress ticking, her hair a neat roll of curls around her head. On her knee is baby Rodney in woolly leggings, his face dark and fierce under the glare of her smile. She turns the pages and pauses at FIRST DAY AT SCHOOL. SEPTEMBER 1946. Thin knees beneath his baggy shorts, little man's haircut, satchel on his shoulder. SUMMER HOLS. SCARBOROUGH 1948. Rodney standing on the promenade in his knitted bathing suit, his hand shading his eyes, unsmiling, a puzzled look on a face that was so like Jim's . . .

She snaps the album shut and sips her coffee, shuddering at the cool skin that clings to her lip. She thinks of Rodney's little boy's body in the woolly swimsuit. How he used to complain! Itchy he said it was, but he had no choice. She'd unravelled a pullover to make it, and worked her fingers to the bone, sitting up late at night to get it finished for the holiday, and she was blethered if he wasn't going to get some wear out of it. He was only eight then. He was still her boy then. His room is ready for him upstairs. It has been ready for him since he was seventeen. And now he is back and there is not a single excuse for her reluctance. She is his mother after all. She knows what Jim would say. But it is time for shopping now. Later there will be time to think.

* * *

Arthur's fingers probe the earth, earth that he has dug and dug again and forked and fed and raked until it is the finest, cleanest tilth in England. His fingers tell him the temperature is right and he pushes the flattish, wrinkled broad-bean seeds into the soil. He likes to poke them in with his finger, so, just down to the second joint, and then cover them with the lovely blanket of the earth. It gives him satisfaction to bed them so comfortably. It is the time, the best time, just before full moon. There is no way that seeds treated so, to the luxury of Arthur's earth, to the full waxing of the moon, will not flourish. Arthur puts his hand in his pocket when he has finished, just to make sure, and squeezes the godstone, warm from his body, in his earthy palm. He stands and surveys the neat job – the earth so brown and even, not a lump or a stone to be seen – and a bubble of pride, of love, swells and bursts in his breast.

He looks up from his own plot to the other variously cultivated rectangles that slope down to the shallow busy river and the park beyond. The allotments are south-facing, perfectly positioned, but some of them are tatty now, neglected. It's not like it was when it was a case of 'grow or go without'. Oh, people are keen now, as ever, but there's not the same pride, the same commitment. There's not the love. There is rubbish tangled among the dying stalks at this dying time of the year, polythene rags tangled on thorns; there are weeds, nettles and the ballooning heads of onions gone to seed.

Once Arthur had dreamt of a time when the land would be composed of industrial villages, where the workers would divide their labour between the factory and the land. He had sweated his own days away in the blasting heat of molten steel and laboured on the soil in the cool of the evenings – and it had meant something. Not just an old man's pottering, a harmless hobby. But somehow, after the war, after the terrible grieving time, the core of his ambition had been lost, as if a bright glow in him had cooled to grey. He had continued just the same, his body performing the same actions, but the original motive, the dreams of change, had gone. Arthur remembers the youth that he was as if he were someone else, someone he had once known and admired and lost. And now he is an old man. Quite content. It hasn't been a bad life, all in all. Just an ordinary one.

Jim's plot is going to waste now. It's next to Arthur's and the two men used to work side by side on the soil, and Arthur misses Jim now, simply misses him. He remembers the arguments they had. Politics. It was always politics. Arthur smiles wryly. He knows that he was right and Jim was wrong; but Jim is dead now and Arthur will be before long, and then it will be all the same, will all have been the same for the both of them. The politics got in the way – but there was a sort of friendship between them. There was the love of the soil that they shared, the love of the green growth that came from their own labour. There was something between Olive and Jim once, around the time of the war. Arthur knew it and he didn't object. How could he? There were others for him, too. That had been their way, Arthur and Olive. They were free. They chose to live together and they were free. They were happy and no one was ever hurt, it had been the right way for them. It was Jim who felt the guilt about his episode with Olive; and Arthur, amusement at his guilt. For Arthur was secure. There was never any danger of Jim coming between himself and Olive. The thought of Olive and Jim, such opposites, was even faintly comic. And they had never spoken of it. Oh no. For Jim was the sort who rarely talked about women or feelings. He worried a bit about the state Nell got into over Rodney, but mostly it was politics they talked about, and club-root and aphids, and they shared a pipe of tobacco over the boundary. But they never mentioned Olive, not more than in passing. And they never spoke away from the allotments, never more than nodded in the street, for Nell had taken against Olive and forbidden Jim to have anything to do with the pair of them. And Jim was weak in that way, a slave to the woman.

Now Jim's plot is a sad tangle. A young couple did take it on and came every Saturday for a month or two while the weather was fine – and then gave it up. Results too slow. It was a sin. A good plot, the sort of earth that only comes from years of toil, of love, going to waste. He would take it on himself, but how can he now? He has neither the time nor the strength. His own allotment is as much as he can manage now with Olive as she is. He sighs. That is the way it is going now that they are so old. He looks up at the sky. The distant white cumulus clouds of the morning have darkened, clustered closer to the earth, and in the air is the smell of approaching rain, and the low stirring of a preliminary breeze. Arthur looks regretfully at the turnips and parsnips that he's yet to lift, at the tidying that wants doing. There's a good day's work there yet, but he knows in his bones that he ought to pack it in. He is not as strong as he was. There are pains in his knees that are worse in the cold and the wet. The first spots of rain flick the leaves. Best, anyway, to get back to Olive.

Three

By the time Olive has managed to force her old tweed coat shut across her chest, comb her hair, apply a slash of scarlet lipstick to her mouth and perch the cherry hat upon her head, the sky is already darkening. Kropotkin sees the lead in her hand, and understanding its promise he leaps at her, so ecstatic that she swallows her fear. It is not a proper fear, it has no particular object, it is just a vague dread of what might be, could be, outside the walls.

She fumbles to attach the lead to Potkins's collar, lost in the curly hair on his neck. It is a fiddly thing, a metal thing that is hard against her fingers.

'Stay still Potkins!' she says. Oh, it is so difficult to bend these days. 'Artie,' she calls, for what is *she* doing struggling like this when he is perfectly capable? And then she remembers. Artie is out on his allotment. Why is it so hard to remember?

As soon as Kropotkin is attached he begins to pull. He pulls her down the passage and out onto the front path, and almost pulls her over. He pulls one way; she had thought to go the other.

'Potty! You bad boy!' she gasps, but he strains his plump wagging body forward regardless and she gives in, stumbles after him. She cannot remember the last time she went out alone, without Arthur to lean upon. Together, they go up to the Lamb every Sunday dinner-time for a glass of stout while the dinner's cooking, but it is months since she ventured out alone. It must be months. It might even be a year.

Wrath Road is a flat road, but it is set in a network of hills and, to reach the shops or the park, a plunge down and then a

long haul up is required, and Olive has simply given up
trying. The hills tilt more steeply than they did in her youth
when she strode up them regardless, or even did the climb on
her bicycle, standing almost still on her pedals on the steepest
bits, attracting the glances of passers-by: a beautiful girl,
slim, black-haired and scarlet-cheeked. A healthy girl. She
holds her chin up, remembering, and her jaw trembles – a
new problem. She is impatient with her old bag of a body.
Inside, when all is clear, she is the same. Through the middle
there is a sliver of that same girl like the writing in a stick of
seaside rock. Now Kropotkin ceases to pull and squats in the
middle of the path, crapping. A passing man mutters something and looks askance at Olive. She gives him her most
brazen look.

When Kropotkin has finished he sniffs in the gutter eagerly,
but there is nothing for him, just tufty grass growing in cracks
and bits of old orange peel dropped by the dustmen.

Petra comes along behind them with the little boy with the
fierce name. He pauses to wipe his shoe on the kerb. 'Hello,'
Petra says. 'Taking the dog for a walk?'

Olive frowns at her. She has never had time for small talk,
not useless talk like that.

'Is that dog the one what barks at my bedtime?' the boy asks.

'Wolfe!' says Olive, triumphantly remembering the boy.
There are kids everywhere these days, hard to remember, hard
to tell them apart. Wolfe looks at her expectantly, but her eyes
switch away.

'We're popping down for some bread and things,' Petra
says. 'Can we fetch you anything while we're at it?'

Olive considers. Chocolate would be nice, but she has no
money. Never mind. Artie will pay when he gets back.
'Chocolate,' she says. 'Milk chocolate, and Artie will put the
money through your door.'

Potkins snuffles up to Wolfe, who looks nervously at the

dog. 'He won't hurt you,' Olive says. 'He's friendly. He only wants to play.' Wolfe doesn't look convinced.

'Hello!' says Petra, suddenly, looking past Olive. Olive looks round and sees Nell. 'We're all out and about this morning.'

'Almost lunch-time I'd call it,' Nell grumbles, taking in Olive, and Kropotkin's business, with one sharp glance. 'Can't stop now. Lots to do.' And she hurries off, her hard heels clacking on the pavement.

'Old slag,' Olive calls after her.

'Well, we must get on,' Petra says. 'A big bar? Cadbury's?'

'Yes.'

'Be seeing you then.' Petra grabs Wolfe's hand and hurries him away. Olive can hear his piping voice drifting back as Petra whips him round the corner: 'Mum, what's a slag?' and she chuckles.

At the corner, Olive tries to stop. She does not intend to go down the hill. It is too steep, the houses at the bottom impossibly far away, impossibly tiny. She stops and holds onto a fence post, but Kropotkin is determined to go down. He pulls and strains, panting and slavering as the collar bites into his neck. His eyes bulge. Olive is afraid that he will do himself a mischief but she can't let him go, for he would be sure to get knocked down by a car, or lost, or stolen; yet if she doesn't she'll have to go with him down the impossible hill. It's all right for some, she thinks, for Nell, only a few months younger, has gone briskly down and will be back later, bags full, balanced like a milkmaid. No, thinks Olive spitefully, not a milkmaid, more like a scarecrow with her scraggy frame. But there is no good thinking it, it is not true. Nell is immaculate. She has been all her life. Her neat grey curls cling to her head like sculptured stone, her coat is brushed, her shoes polished, her stockings smooth. Even the wrinkles on her face occur symmetrically. 'No, I am the scarecrow,' Olive mutters. She can see her reflection in window of a house. I am the scarecrow, fat and wispy in my cherry hat. She wants to cry out that it is not true, that she is beautiful. *Beautiful*, wild and rosy. She is not really a dumpy old bag with a trembling chin. Not really.

And Kropotkin will not give it up. He tugs hard and in the end Olive's fingers, numb from the strain, give way and he is off, a fat torpedo down the hill. He chases a tabby cat with a white streak down its back like a spine. Olive rubs one poor hand with the other. Her fingers are trembling with the fright and the strain. She will have to follow Potkins. It is no good. She cannot let him go. Whatever would Arthur say? 'Oh Artie!' she moans, 'this is your fault. It is. You will go out and leave me. Selfish, you are. Selfish.' And all around the windows of the houses glint at her blindly and no one has seen her predicament, no one helps or cares. 'Potkins,' she calls, and she begins to stumble down the hill. She holds onto her hat with one hand and grasps the wall with the other for support. She has not been down here for months, not for years, down here past the hydrangeas and the privet that grows in the narrow strip between the walls, with their stumps of iron palings, and the windows.

Kropotkin had disappeared between the parked cars, and Olive hurries, almost running now, panting. Fear clutches at her, and her heart scrambles madly in her chest. Her face is wet, for she is crying.

'Potkins!' she calls, louder, and then she sees him, darting between two parked cars and out into the road. She reaches forward and then she trips and falls with a great fat wallop onto the pavement. At once Potkins is back, he is upon her licking her cheek and enveloping her in clouds of his doggy breath.

'All right, missus? Come on, upsy-daisy,' and she is hauled to her feet by two youths.

'Are you all right?' they keep saying. She is humiliated. No, she is not all right. She is far from all right. Her knees burn and her hands where they smacked the pavement. Tears run down her cheeks.

'We'll walk you home,' one of them says. 'This your dog?'

Olive points the way up the hill and the young men, who are good young men, take Olive's arms, one each, and one of them hangs onto Potkins who continues to pull, and they walk slowly together back up the hill. They leave Olive at her door, offering to call a doctor, or fetch a neighbour in to help, but Olive shakes her head. 'No thank you,' she manages to say. 'All right now. All better. Thank you.'

'Well if you're sure . . .' and they go off, looking doubtful and awkward and young. Olive leaves Potkins in the yard with his lead on for she can't be doing with all that fiddling now, not with her fingers so sore. Once inside, she makes the mistake of looking in Arthur's shaving mirror, a mottled square above the sink, and she discovers that her face is red and swollen, the lipstick a grotesque smear on her chin – and that the hat has gone. It must have come off when she fell – her best hat, her only hat, the cherry hat that suited her so well. Olive sits down on the stairs, her coat straining under her arms, her knees and the palms of her hands smarting, and she weeps. Chairman Mao creeps downstairs and onto her lap. Her tears drip onto the bluish skin of his back and he purrs and his claws go in and out rhythmically, catching in the threads of her coat.

* * *

Nell tuts at the prices. In her wire basket she has a small bran-enriched loaf, a small tub of margarine, one bottle of disinfectant and one of bleach, and now she queues for her quarter of cheese. It is the nice assistant on the cheese counter today, she notices gratefully, the one who doesn't object to slicing small pieces of cheese for an old woman.

Ahead of her in the queue is a shuffling old woman, the sagging type, the type who has let herself go, surrendered to gravity – like Olive. This morning is the first time that Nell has been face to face with Olive for quite some time. Satisfaction stirs in her breast and a tight smile puckers her lips. She hated Olive, even as they shared the same desk at school, even as she went to tea at her house, masquerading as her little friend. Olive was not quite nice, not quite suitable in Nell's eyes, not that her family weren't a nice family, for although her mother fancied herself an artist, her father worked for the Post Office. But Olive was wild. She had a loud laugh, a really shocking laugh, suggestive, not ladylike at all. And she had a wide red mouth and her eyes were almost black, they sparkled blackly, indecently, not like English eyes; and her cheeks were bright as poppies. She had nice clothes, always nicely made, but she always looked a mess, hair escaping from her plait, stockings wrinkled, sash twisted, a splash of something on her front. It drove Nell mad that it didn't seem to matter. Nobody minded if Olive was a mess. Nell pats her perm. She always took such care to be a lady. And she was quite pretty enough too, in her way, in her quiet, decent, English way. She had pale brown hair, and pale blue eyes – like harebells Jim had said – and her skin was fair. She always had a tiny waist, and trim it is still, and her ankles still fine and bony. She smirks at the memory of Olive's socks, and fat bare legs above them. Oh, she might have been a beauty once, Olive Owens, but now she is a fright.

Nell buys some eggs and half a cucumber, a morsel of frozen smoked haddock and two small bananas, and then, as a gesture towards Rodney, she chooses a box of iced fancies: yellow, pink and chocolate diamonds, spangled with jellied fruit. By the time she's finished in the supermarket, the rain has started to fall. Nell is well prepared, always one step ahead of any eventuality. She wears her mac over an extra cardigan, and now she unfolds a transparent plastic rain-hat, arranges it over her curls and ties it neatly under her chin.

Nell toils up the hill. She takes it easy. Twenty-five steps and then a pause. Jim used to joke about the hill, say it kept her trim. Oh, but he was a gentleman. He would carry her bags up the hill for her, without a second thought, and even push little Rodney in his pram – very unusual for a man in those days. You see them all over now, men pushing babies in those flimsy little buggers or whatever they call them, something new-fangled and American. Buggies.

Half-way up the hill, as she pauses on a twenty-fifth step, Nell notices something unexpected in the gutter, under a parked car. She rests her shopping basket and her plastic carrier-bag on the ground for a moment as she looks. It is a hat. It is not just any old hat, it is familiar. It is a black straw hat, quite a nice hat really except for some silly wax cherries on the side, common, like sucked sweets. It looks just like Olive's hat, the hat she's had for donkey's years, the hat that she was wearing this morning – ridiculous old tart that she is. Nell experiences a little swoop of excitement. What a dilemma! She'd like to pick the hat up and take it home. Before she gives it back, of course. For it must be returned to Olive. But it would be humiliating to be caught crouching down and putting her hand in the gutter, under a filthy car, which is what she will have to do in order to reach it. She looks up and down the hill. Nobody about. She looks at the rows of windows. Nobody, apparently, looking out. Quickly she stoops down and pulls out the hat from beneath the car. The blood rushes to her head as she leans over and she can hear her pulse. She jams the hat into her carrier-bag without even pausing to examine it and continues up the hill, her cheeks pink, and in her excitement manages the rest of the hill without counting her steps.

* * *

On the stairs, Olive weeps for her hat. Arthur gave her the hat
in 1945 to celebrate the end of the war. Miraculously, for it
was certainly not a cheap hat and he had no money, and he
might even, Olive suspects, have stolen it, but that doesn't
matter. It is a beautiful hat, a celebration hat, and it might have
been made for her, he had said, made for a beauty with cherry
lips and ebony eyes, made for his Olive. She weeps for the hat,
and she weeps for her sore hands and knees, and she weeps
because she has done something shameful. She has peed on the
stairs. She couldn't help it. It just wouldn't stop, she just
couldn't stop it, not sitting crouched forward at the bottom of
the stairs. She weeps for Arthur, for what he will think of her,
and on her lap, curled into a bony ball, slumbers Mao.

* * *

Wolfe throws scraps of bread to the ducks. Poor ducks. It is
raining and it is cold. The green pond-water is spotted with the
holes and the circles the raindrops make. Poor ducks who have
to sit in the cold water all day, all night, all winter.

'Come on,' says Petra. 'We'll get soaked to the skin.'

'Just a minute,' Wolfe says. He is trying to toss his last scrap of
bread to one of the brown ducks that hasn't had any yet, but a
greedy green one snaps it up first. 'Horrible duck!' Wolfe shouts.

'I'm going,' Petra says, and she turns her back and walks
away. Wolfe trails along behind, dragging his shoes through
the wet leaves. It is a good park. There's the river running
through, the allotments up one side, some swings and a see-
saw, and lots of grey squirrels amongst the trees.

'There's plenty of sticks,' Wolfe calls. 'We need some sticks
for the bonfire.'

'Not now though,' Petra turns and holds out her hand. 'They're too wet. Come on, let's get back and have lunch. Bob and Buff will be wondering where we've got to.'

'Could we get an allotment?' Wolfe asks, taking her hand. 'Then we could grow all sorts of things.'

Petra pauses and squints through the rain, up at the drenched plots. 'That's a thought,' she says. 'It depends.'

'On Tom?'

'No!'

'What then?'

'I keep trying to explain . . . I just don't know.'

Wolfe tries to stop it, but a hot tear squeezes out and joins the raindrops running down his face. 'I don't like it, Mum,' he says. 'I don't like not being sure.'

'Nor do I,' Petra says. They have reached the park gates. 'Come on, let's hurry home. Look, I promise I'll get it sorted soon.'

'How?'

'I don't know. But the baby will be here soon, and Tom and I will have to make some decisions, and then we'll know whether we're coming or going. Now we've got to climb this ruddy hill so shut up and save your breath.'

They climb the hill in silence. The rainwater flows in the gutter like a river and the drops splat so hard on the pavement that they send up little round splashes. Petra's hair trails down like wet string. Wolfe's socks are soggy. He stops crying and wipes his nose on the sleeve of his anorak.

'Ducks can't smile, can they?' he says suddenly.

Petra pauses. 'No, I don't suppose they can!' she laughs and squeezes his hand. He turns and looks down the hill. He sees Arthur.

'Look, there's that man from next door,' he says.

Petra turns, and they wait. 'Hello,' Petra says as he catches them up, 'you look nearly as wet as us!'

Arthur grimaces. 'Thought to get moving on allotment, but rain put paid to that.'

'I'd like an allotment,' Wolfe says, 'but we're in a state of flux. I might plant a tree though, mightn't I, Mum? In the garden.'

'Good for you, lad,' Arthur chuckles. 'What sort of tree?'

'Don't know yet. I'm still considering.'

Arthur smiles at Petra in the way that adults smile at each other over children's heads, but Wolfe doesn't mind. He likes the way Arthur's wrinkles crinkle round his eyes, and likes his shaggy eyebrows and the way the raindrops hang on the brim of his cap.

'You can always come up allotment with me if you like,' Arthur says. 'I could do with a hand. If it's all right with your mum.'

'Can I?' Wolfe begs. 'Please Mum. I could take my trowel. I've got a trowel. I used to have my own bit of garden at the Longhouse,' he explains. 'I used to grow the very best radishes in the world.'

'Of course he can, if you're sure he won't be a nuisance . . .' Petra says.

'Tomorrow?' asks Wolfe.

'I'll let you know, lad. It might be a day or two.'

'Great,' says Wolfe. 'That's just great.' Arthur is lovely. He is like a grandpa. He will be someone to talk to. Timidly, Wolfe takes his hand and Arthur looks down oddly at him, almost sadly.

'Oh, we bought some chocolate for your . . .' Petra takes it out of her bag.

Arthur smiles. 'She's a devil for it,' he says, 'always has been always will be.'

They have reached the top of the hill. Petra stops and rests for a moment. 'I won't be able to do that for much longer,' she says, her hand on her belly.

'When's it due?' Arthur asks.

'End of the month.'

'Not so long then. What do you want?' Arthur asks Wolfe, 'a brother or a sister?'

'Don't really mind,' says Wolfe.

'There's a lad,' says Arthur, squeezing his hand.

* * *

As soon as he gets through the back gate, Arthur can tell that something is wrong. Kropotkin is out in the rain, sodden and bedraggled, for the outhouse door is shut. His lead still trails from his neck.

'Poor old boy,' Arthur says. He takes off the lead and opens the door so that the dog can get into his basket. He is almost afraid to go into the house, and as soon as he does, he can hear Olive crying.

'There, there, me duck,' he says, finding her bundled in her coat at the bottom of the stairs. 'It's all right, me old love. What's up? Tell me what's up.'

'Oh Artie,' wails Olive. 'Oh Artie . . . oh it's awful out there. My hat, oh my cherry hat.'

'Come on,' says Arthur. 'Let's get you up and get your coat off.'

'But you don't understand . . . my hat, Artie, I've lost my hat.'

'Come on, it's not end of world . . .' Arthur tries to pull her up but Olive resists. She will not meet his eyes.

'And I've peed myself,' she whispers. 'I'm sorry, Artie. I'm so sorry. I just couldn't move. I couldn't help it.'

'That's all right, Ollie,' Arthur says. 'Come on, love.' He struggles her into an upright position. His heart beats wildly with the strain and the anxiety. 'Oh my poor love. What about a bath, eh? A nice warm bath.'

'If you think that would be best, Artie.'

'Let's dry your eyes first,' he says, and with his old handkerchief, warm and crumpled from his pocket, he wipes away her tears and the smudge of her lipstick. 'Now, can you sit there a minute?' he manoeuvres her onto a kitchen chair. She sits down painfully, obediently. 'It's just for a moment. I'll pour you a drop of brandy, then I'll run bath.'

Olive submits. She sits on the stiff chair, her spine aching and the back of her dress cold and wet against her legs. She sips the brandy and listens to the comforting sound of the water flowing into the bath upstairs. Mao tries to creep back onto her lap but she pushes him off. He is too sharp, too cold. She isn't in the mood for Mao, now. The brandy leaves a trail of gold from her tongue, down her throat and into her belly, a hot trail that spreads and seeps through her until the spasms of her weeping subside.

* * *

Nell sits in her armchair. On the coffee table beside her are a cucumber sandwich, a banana and a cup of tea – her lunch. She has switched the television news on for a bit of company, but her eyes are not on the flickering screen, her eyes are on the hat. It sits on the other chair, Jim's chair, a splash of brightness in the beige of the room.

As she chews her sandwich – thirty chews per mouthful, Jim's recipe for a good digestion and though he had his troubles his stomach was never among them – Nell considers Olive's hat, and considers Olive. They used to sit together at school all that time ago, both clever girls, the top of the class. Only, of course, they couldn't both be top. Olive was always slightly sharper with arithmetic while Nell's spelling was flawless. They were best friends, 'soul mates' her father called it, approving of Olive. He encouraged the supposed friendship, urged Nell to invite Olive on family outings where she would outshine everyone, sparkle indecently, until, Nell suspected, her father preferred Olive to herself. Olive used to lark about with Edwin too, and Father didn't mind that and it simply wasn't fair because Nell had to sit and be quiet and still, seen but not heard, while Olive could make as much of a commotion as she liked, joke and laugh and torment Edwin till he blushed. 'She's a proper card!' Father used to laugh. 'And those eyes! My God. Gypsy eyes they are. You mark my word, bees round a honeypot when she's a few years older. You see if I'm not right.' And he started to call her Gypsy Rose, Gypsy for short, and Olive loved it, used to play up to him, all pert and flirting and flashing her eyes in a way she never bothered with at school, while Nell glowered. He never had a pet name for her. He called her Eleanor and she had to be neat and prim, still and quiet as a pink and white china doll with painted-on eyes and a sweet stiff face. He would have been furious if his Eleanor had behaved like Olive, like his little Gypsy. He was tickled by Nell's cleverness at school, but didn't think it a serious matter. He didn't pay attention to her reports in the same way he did Edwin's. Edwin's brains mattered more even though Nell was brighter. In her autograph book, he wrote once, the day after she'd come top in a mental arithmetic test – beating Olive by a clear three points – '*Be good sweet maid, and let who will be clever.*'

Despite Nell's spelling and her occasional ability to beat Olive at arithmetic, it was Olive who came out top of the class in their final year at school. Nell still remembers that failure, *not* a failure everyone said, someone had to win, but that is how it felt. On the day they had to write their composition, Nell had been indisposed. She had had her period and she had had crampy pains and felt dizzy and sick but she hadn't said, she'd just soldiered on. One didn't make a song and dance of it in those days, not like today, she thinks, when it's emblazoned

everywhere, advertisments for stick-ons and stick-ups all over
the place. Filthy it is, and you can't get away from it: switch on
the television, open a magazine and there it is. There's no
proper sense of shame any more. People use it as an excuse
now, you can do anything – murder – and get away with it
these days, but then you just kept quiet and battled on and
back luck if it happened to be an important day.

She remembers writing. She even remembers the title of the
composition: *Poets are the Trumpets that Sing to Battle.
Discuss.* She remembers the clock ticking, the scraping of
many pens, the way Olive's pen flew. And she remembers the
dark sinister leaking between her legs. And Olive had come out
top of the class. She had won the prize. It was a little cup, a nice
little cup like a silver vase, engraved with her name and the
date, and one other word: EXCELLENCE. And Olive went up on
the stage, her sash all awry, ink on her blouse, to receive the
cup. It made Nell want to spit. And now Olive is a fat old
spinster, childless, senile. Oh excellent! At least Nell has a son,
at least Nell hasn't gone to seed. She finishes her tea and peels
her banana and gloats over Olive's hat.

Four

The bathroom is dim and steamy. Drips of condensation run down the walls and outside the rain beats against the frosted window-glass. Olive is squeezed into the bath, and Arthur sits on the toilet lid watching her. Her eyes are closed and she looks dead and yellow. Her breasts have slipped down her sides. Her big purplish hands rest on her belly above the sparse white tufts of hair. *It used to be such a curling bush, so black, so rosy pink beneath.* Her thighs are massive, and on each of her knees is an ugly graze.

'We'll have to patch up those knees, Ollie,' he says. 'Lucky you broke nothing. You must have gone down a smack.'

'I did, Artie.' She opens her eyes a slit, and he is relieved. She looks more like his Olive, with her eyes open.

'Let's get you washed,' he says. He kneels down beside the bath and takes the bar of lavender soap and rubs it between his hard palms. He rubs the sparkling froth of bubbles into Olive's front from her neck to her belly. He closes his eyes, enjoying the slip of his hands against her flesh. 'Remember how we used to . . .'

'Remember how! And how I soaped your back. We'd never fit in together. Not now.' Olive looks down at her fatness.

'Slippery fingers.' Arthur slips his hands round and soaps her lolling breasts. 'My old love,' he murmurs. He soaps her legs, between her toes, her thighs, and around underneath in the tender soapy crevices. *And oh she was passionate and she would never lie still, not like the others, never let him take control.*

'I saw Nell this morning,' Olive says suddenly, her eyes open wide. He feels her stiffen. 'Looked at me as if I was shit. As if I care. Buggering slag.'

'Ollie. Be calm. And anyone less of a slag . . .'

'That's right, defend her! And where were you, Artie, while I was out there alone?'

'Think, Ollie. Come on now, remember.' Arthur is frightened by the way her memory is failing, anxious and also impatient. He cannot believe that she can really be so forgetful. Surely she does it on purpose, sometimes, to be awkward, for she has always been awkward, Olive has, never an easy person to live with.

Olive shrugs. She clutches his hand. 'I want my hat.'

'Come on lass, lean forward and I'll do your back . . . I'll go out and look in a bit. It'll be there somewhere. I'll wait while rain stops. I met young woman from next door again on my way up hill. Nice little lad, little fat lad.'

'Some odd name. Not the fashion. An animal name.'

'But a grand lad.'

Arthur helps her out of the bath and dries her. There is something wholesome and lovely about her, clean and fat. He pats lavender talc under her arms and under her breasts and between her thighs where they rub together. Her sallow skin glows pink from the warmth of the water, from the rubbing of his soapy hands. He chooses clean clothes for her. It is comforting to comfort her. He rubs Germolene into the grazes on her knees and hands, and patches them with neat squares of gauze.

'There, there,' he soothes, then together they go downstairs, for it is past dinner-time, and they eat ham sandwiches and dip Garibaldis in their tea.

'Dead-fly biscuits,' Olive remembers, as she always does. 'I'd not touch them as a lass.'

Arthur looks lovingly at her. She is all right now. Her cheeks are rosy again from the fire, her clean hair is a fluffy halo. 'Good as new,' he says.

*　　*　　*

Petra empties two tins of tomato soup into a saucepan. 'Call the others,' she says to Wolfe. Wolfe goes to the bottom of the stairs.

'Ready,' he calls.

'Could you get some bowls out?' Petra says.

'Mum, can we ask Arthur round when we have our bonfire?' Wolfe asks, taking four bowls off the draining board and putting them on the table.

'Oh I don't know . . . and some spoons.'

'Why not?'

'I just don't think he'd appreciate it.'

'He could always say no.'

'I suppose so. Put the bread on the table would you? And give Bob and Buff another shout.'

'Ready!' shouts Wolfe. 'So can we?'

Petra comes to the table and pours the bright orange soup into the bowls. 'We couldn't just ask *him*. We'd have to ask Olive too.'

'So?'

Petra goes to the bottom of the stairs. 'Ready!' she cries, and Bobby comes thundering down.

Wolfe sits down at the table and sighs.

'We're making a guy,' Bobby says, dipping a slice of bread into his soup.

'We haven't got a fire yet,' Wolfe points out.

'Doesn't take a minute to chuck a few bits of wood together.'

'What bits of wood?' asks Petra. 'I'll tell you what, Wolfe: why not ask Arthur if he's got anything we can burn?'

'We could ask that old bat the other side too,' Bobby says.

'What's Buffy doing?' complains Petra, looking at the cooling bowl of soup.

'She went out,' Bobby says.

'Well you could have said. Where's she gone?'

'Search me. Here she comes, anyhow.'

The gate bangs, and Buffy comes through the door, her hair wet and spiky. 'Hi,' she says. 'Lunch. Great.' She walks straight through the room and, still wrapped in her baggy coat, goes up the stairs.

'Oi!' calls Petra.

'Just a minute.'

'What's she up to?' mutters Petra.

'Can I have her soup?' asks Bobby.

Petra frowns at him. Buffy comes downstairs, sheds her coat and tucks into her lunch. Wolfe wipes a slice of bread round his bowl. The soup is sweet and smooth and delicious. They never had tinned soup at the Longhouse. It was usually lentil and full of ragged chunks of turnip. But still, despite the soup it would be nice to be there. Everyone would help with the bonfire there and it would be gigantic.

'I'll only go and ask Arthur if he's got any wood if I can invite him,' he says to Petra.

She pushes her still-damp hair back from her face and smiles at him. 'Oh all right. Maybe I'll invite that side too,' she says. 'The more the merrier. She might be offended if she sees we've invited Olive and Arthur and not her.' She switches her gaze to Buffy. 'And what did you have hidden under your coat?'

'Nothing.'

'Oh no . . .' she begins but the gate bangs again. Wolfe sees a dark curly head.

'It's Tom!' he cries.

'Wotcha,' says Tom. 'Hello mate.' He rubs Wolfe's head.

'Didn't expect you,' says Petra, getting up. 'I'll make some tea.'

Tom sits down on her chair and throws a carrier-bag on the table.

'What is it?' asks Buffy.

'Take a look.' Buffy grabs it before Wolfe can reach and pulls out an oblong box.

'Fireworks!' shrieks Wolfe. 'Let me see! Let me see!'

'Let Wolfie look,' says Petra. 'Anything to eat, Tom?'

'Just because he's the youngest,' complains Buffy, slinging the box at Wolfe. He opens it carefully and is the first to sniff the gunpowdery smell.

'Brilliant!' he breathes. The box is packed with fat paper tubes and cones and coils. 'Traffic Lights,' he reads. 'Golden Rain. Vesuvius. Shattering Star. Look at this rocket! Red Arrow . . . and sparklers!' It is like a box of treasure. He fingers each one.

'Be careful or you'll bust them,' Bobby says. 'What *was* under your coat, Buffy?'

'Shut up,' Buffy says. 'Let me look now.' She snatches the box away.

'Remember Jumping Jacks?' Tom asks Petra. She brings the teapot to the table and Wolfe sees him stroke her bottom.

'They used to chase you round the garden!' Petra laughs. 'I nearly got one in my wellie once. Terrifying.'

Petra stoops and kisses the top of Tom's head. Wolfe shrugs. He wishes they'd make up their minds whether they're still in love or not. He hears a funny scritchy-scratchy noise.

'What's that noise?' he asks.

'What noise?'

'Listen.'

They are all quiet and they all hear the noise.

'Oh heck,' says Buffy. Wolfe opens the door and a tiny black kitten tumbles into the room. It give a high-pitched miaow and totters on its wobbly legs towards the table.

'Nothing?' says Petra, looking accusingly at Buffy. 'I thought we agreed. No pets.'

Buffy picks the kitten up and buries her nose in its fur. She mutters something inaudible.

'Pardon?'

'Tom said no pets, not you. And he's never here. I thought you'd split up.'

Tom pulls a face. He gets out his tobacco and papers and busies himself rolling a cigarette.

'That's got nothing to do with it,' Petra says. 'You can't just go getting a pet without consulting me.'

'You never consulted me about the baby!' mumbles Buffy.

Petra flushes and looks as if she might cry. Tom gives Buffy a filthy look and pours Petra some tea.

'Sorry,' mumbles Buffy.

'What shall we call it?' Wolfe asks helpfully. The kitten blinks at him with its green marble eyes, and lashes its pipe-cleaner tail.

'Nothing,' says Tom, lighting his cigarette, 'because you're not keeping it.'

'That's quite a good name,' says Wolfe.

'What, "Nothing"?' Bobby scoffs. 'You can't call it that. Let's call it Skull.'

'You can go and take it back, now,' says Tom.

'Can't,' says Buffy. 'Or she'll be drowned. Do you want her to be drowned?'

'Not my problem.'

'We'll have to find it a new home,' says Petra wearily. 'And in the mean time, I don't think you should call it anything.'

'All right then,' Buffy retorts, 'I won't call her Anything. I'll call her Nothing.'

'You'll feel bloody stupid standing on the doorstep at night calling, "Nothing," ' grumbles Bobby.

'Come on, Nothing,' Buffy carries the kitten away upstairs, murmuring to her as she goes.

'I'm going to get on with the guy,' Bobby says, and follows her.

'Sorry,' Petra says to Tom. Wolfe frowns at her. He can't see what she's got to be sorry about.

'You all right?' Tom asks her.

'Just tired.'

'I'll tell you what, mate,' Tom says to Wolfe. 'Why don't you come into town with me tomorrow? I'm going to do a picture.'

'On the pavement!'

Tom is a street artist, and he's never taken Wolfe with him before. It hasn't been fair because he's taken the others, but never Wolfe. He usually gets left with Petra.

'That would be great! Can I Mum?'

'Course you can.'

'What about a lie-down now,' Tom asks. 'I could do with a kip myself.'

Petra smiles down at her tea, and nods.

'All right, me old mate?' Tom says. 'Can you keep yourself amused for an hour? Watch the box, or something.'

Wolfe nods. Petra and Tom go upstairs together. Wolfe gets the box of fireworks and takes them all out and arranges them on the table. 'Golden Rain. Traffic Lights. Snakes of Fire,' he whispers. 'Vesuvius. Red Arrow. Shattering Star.'

* * *

Nell goes up the stairs for her afternoon rest. She takes the hat up with her, and puts it on Jim's pillow, beside her.

'See Jim,' she says. 'See what I found.'

'It's hers,' Jim replies. 'What do you mean "found"?'

'I did really, on the street. She must have dropped it.'

'Nell, we don't want that performance all over again. You must give it back.'

'Hush,' says Nell. 'I must get some shut-eye. Didn't sleep a wink last night.'

She folds back her eiderdown and settles herself down. She

lies on her back, stockinged feet neatly together, toes pointing
to the ceiling, eyes closed. There is so much to worry her
nowadays, it's a wonder she sleeps at all. There's Rodney.
What should she do about Rodney? A good mother would
welcome him back, glad to be able to keep an eye on him, and
Nell is nothing if not a good mother.

As she drowses, she remembers bombs, the whine and hiss
of bombs, brilliant flowering explosions in a frosty night sky,
brighter than the full moon and the stars. There is the rattle of
machine-gun fire, like hail upon glass, and there are flames that
make the city spread out below glow red and almost
glamorous. She is a young mother and her baby son clings to
her, terrified. Jim is away watching bombs fall from a foreign
sky, same moon, same stars; and his baby, baby Rodney,
clings to her. She carries him down the stairs and in a daze, a
strange state in which she appreciates the beauty of the bombs
and the blazing city, she carries him out into the loud and
smoky air and into the Anderson shelter where it is cold and
mushroomy-dark and almost quiet, and she rocks him to
sleep. She is a good mother and her child loosens his clutch on
her coat as his breathing deepens and he grows heavy in her
arms. Little Rodney is asleep. She puts him down in the
packing-case cot Jim made for him, and covers him snugly in
blankets. She listens to his breathing, heavy, even, healthy.
And then sits huddled and cold, listening to the muffled war
outside and sucking a fluffy peppermint she found in her coat
pocket. Quite a way away, she thinks comfortingly. They
wouldn't bomb here, not ordinary people like me, not mothers
with babies, not ordinary houses with ordinary people. But, of
course, they would, and they do. There is a high-pitched
squeal. Near. Almost in her ear, like a mosquito, close enough
to swat. And then there is a pause, silence but for the peaceful
rhythm of Rodney's breathing. And then there is a whooshing
thud and the shelter rocks and Nell has to stifle a scream. There

is a close thumping in the earth, a movement, as if it is gathering itself up to spring, and then it subsides. Nell's heart is racing. There is the awful trickle of sweat inside her clothes although she is so cold. Rodney has not even stirred. He sleeps the sleep of the innocent, the trusting. Nell waits she doesn't know how long, a long time, long enough for the sounds of war to recede, like a storm passing over.

And then she has to look. She has to get out and look to see whether it is her house that has been hit, her carpets and curtains and furniture destroyed. She leaves Rodney where he is safe and goes out into the garden. She has to push hard on the door for there is something in the way: slates, slates blown like autumn leaves against the door. She cannot see at first the few feet to the house for the air is thick and sour with smoke and dust. But her house is still there, intact but for a broken window-pane or two and the glass blown out of the back door. She almost weeps with relief – but there is trouble two doors down, at Olive and Arthur's.

The house is standing but there are flames, there is destruction. There is nothing Nell can do to help, not with a baby asleep in the shelter. She goes back inside and closes the door and only hours later, after all-clear, does she step outside again. Her limbs are stiff with the cold and the cramped position she has been sitting in. Outside everywhere, from everywhere, people are calling and shouting, quite jolly some of the voices as if it is some sort of game – and yes, Olive's voice is among them. The fire is out but there is a smoking hole in the back of the house, and the roof is damaged. Nell crunches on glass and broken slates as she carries Rodney into her own safe house. She tucks him into his wooden cot and then she sets to work, sweeping up the broken glass and scrubbing the floor and the window-sills, brushing the carpet to get rid of the dust and the smoky grime. When it is as clean as she can make it, she goes back outside into the raw light of dawn – for she is attracted to destruction.

Olive's things are everywhere, strewn everywhere with the broken bits of her house. In her own garden, Nell finds some odds and ends worth picking up. As she stands out there looking at the dawn-lit ruins of the city, there is a sudden high-pitched ringing and she jumps, her heart spurting painful blood, thoughts of sinister weapons, delayed-action bombs, racing: and then she laughs. It is an alarm clock. Olive and Arthur's alarm clock most likely, flung right across the gardens. It rings insistently despite its shattered glass, and Nell picks it up from among the sharp fragments that litter the ground and switches it off. She slings it over the fence and carries her more important booty back into the house.

Nell smiles and opens her eyes. She is refreshed though she hasn't been to sleep, not properly. She liked the war. She *was* attracted to the destruction and yet it never touched her, not close enough to hurt, close enough only to thrill. She liked the to-do. She liked to make do. She was ingenious, Jim always said afterwards, while food was still rationed. She made meals that would have been a feast in the best of circumstances; she cut down Jim's old shirts and her own frocks and coats and made little clothes for Rodney that wouldn't have looked out of place in Buckingham Palace. She was a brave woman, a smart woman, and she never let Hitler interfere with *her* routine. Never a day without lipstick, not like some who let themselves look like frights as if war was some sort of excuse for sloppiness. She was excused war work because of baby Rodney but still she was an example of what made Britain great, doing her bit to keep it all going, civilian life, in her own small way. That was what Jim said and he knew what was what, being a fighting man himself. She misses the war. She misses the sense of purpose.

She opens her eyes and looks at Jim. 'You're right,' she says and smiles at him fondly. 'I'll have our Rodney back home where he belongs. He *is* our son when all's said and done. He can have his old room back with all his old things.'

Jim smiles at her, pleased, and when he smiles like that it is almost as if sunshine spills out of his frame and into the room. 'That's my Nell,' he says. 'And why not get that hat back to Olive? You'll feel the better for it.'

Nell sits up and puts her feet on the floor. She pauses while her body adjusts to the vertical position. She picks up the hat and then drops it. 'It's got some of her disgusting hair stuck to it. Caught in the straw. Wretched filthy thing. Wants burning. What would I want with it anyway?'

'That's my lass,' says Jim.

* * *

Arthur peers out of the window. 'Rain's stopped,' he remarks. 'I'll get off out and look for hat.'

'You'll find it, won't you Artie?' Olive says.

'If it's there, Ollie, I'll find it.'

'And then everything will be all right again.'

'Mmm.' Olive looks sharply at Arthur. He sounds doubtful. He stoops a little, standing there by the window. He never used to stoop. He used to stand straight, look at the world straight, defiant even. Now, what with his stoop, he looks apologetic.

'Of course it'll be there,' Olive says. 'And what will I do?'

'There's television. There's books. You used to love to read, Ollie. I haven't seen you read for donkey's years.'

'We used to read, didn't we, Artie? The books we read! When we went away, remember Artie? It never mattered where we were you used to say, we might have been on the moon for all the notice we took. Always with our noses stuck in our books!'

'I'll fetch you down some books, Ollie, to look at while you wait.'

'We used to think and talk. We'd read anything. We knew such words! Now when I read, Artie, nothing follows. The whatsits, the joining bits have gone so that nothing follows.'

Arthur smiles at her. 'Wait on,' he says. She listens to him going upstairs, his footsteps jerky and quick. He will go in the back bedroom, a room she hasn't been in for years. No cause to. The floor of that room is all books and boxes, and the boxes themselves mostly full of books. Two complete sets of Dickens; Tolstoy; Shakespeare; Morris; Tennyson; Wordsworth; Yeats – so many millions of printed words all piled there. They liked it like that. It had been very unlike Artie, but she had persuaded him, and he had come round. If the books had been on shelves, as Arthur had wished, they would hardly have looked at them. You get used to books on a shelf, like wallpaper. Piled on the floor there was movement. They'd sit in there and lean upon the books, rest their wine glasses upon the books, make love among the books sometimes when the mood caught them. They'd move them round, flick through the tops of piles, rebuild. She would untidy and Arthur would neaten. They would turn things up they might otherwise have forgotten. She rubs her eyes.

Arthur returns with a little stack of books. 'Are you comfortable?' He puts the books beside her, and helps settle her against a cushion. He turns down the gas fire for the room is warm. He switches on the lamp: 'All right?' He picks some toffee papers up from the floor. 'I'll have to run Ewbank round in here,' he says.

Olive watches him patiently. She does not want to read. There is something the matter with her eyes nowadays and she cannot read for long before the words jump and jumble, and her temples throb. She probably needs glasses but she doesn't want them. She looks awful enough and the world looks awful enough without them both springing into focus. What with the words jumping and the way one idea won't connect with the next, reading is a miserable business, and she gave it up long ago – as Artie well knows.

'Won't be long.' Arthur squeezes her shoulder and leaves her be. She hears him going out of the passage, talking away to Potkins. She listens to the quietness. The gas fire hisses and pings, a car drives past, a child shouts. She looks at the books beside her. What has he chosen? Thomas Hardy, Aldous Huxley – and Arthur's book, the one by Kropotkin that was practically his bible. She opens it and in the lamplight sees that the edges of its pages are furred with dust. Arthur is slipping up. He used to mind about dust; funny that he was so finicky, so particular. And he used to know the book by heart. She has a memory of him standing on the allotment, just a young man, red in the face from digging, a sharp exciting smell of sweat coming from him, making her want him right there. His cupped hands were full of earth. 'Kropotkin talks about the making of earth by gardener,' he said. 'The earth became his, through his work. Do you know that in renting contracts of French allotments, gardener can carry away soil he's made?' Olive remembers shaking her head and squeezing her thighs together as she watched the brown earth trickle between his fingers. Sometimes she'd cycle to the allotment just to make love to him in the shed, quick, hot, grubby love that left earthy fingerprints on the skin under her dress, and then she'd cycle home, pressing her soft wetness against the hard of her saddle, an enigmatic smile upon her face.

She chuckles and shakes her head. They were happy, and they were in love. They were not approved of but nobody could say that they were not happy.

She puts Arthur's book down and picks up *Under the Greenwood Tree*. There is her name in the front: 'Olive Owens, September 1943', in her own handwriting. The book was a birthday gift from Arthur. He had sent it to her from Norfolk. She remembers unwrapping the brown-paper parcel,

and opening the book to begin reading immediately and
finding that Arthur had underlined the first paragraph.

*To dwellers in the wood almost every species of tree
has its voice as well as its feature. At the passing of the
breeze the fir trees sob and moan no less distinctly than
they rock; the holly whistles as it battles with itself; the
ash hisses amid its quiverings; the beech rustles while
its flat boughs rise and fall. And winter, which modifies
the notes of such trees as they shed their leaves, does
not destroy its individuality.*

Olive reads slowly, frowning, her lips moving with the
effort. It meant something once. In the war Arthur had sent it
to her because it meant something to him. Arthur had had to
go away during the war because he refused to fight. Brave man.
And how she had loved him and respected him. He worked on
a farm in Norfolk and he grew passionate about the land. He
met others with the same passion for cultivation and for
comradeship. For years they had been mostly apart. She flicks
through the pages and a dead flat thing, a brownish thing,
flutters out.

It is a petal, the petal of a pressed flower. A rose petal? She
supposes it came from Arthur, but that memory has gone.

In the years before the war he was full of fire. *Mein Kampf*
had been published and people were reading it and Arthur said
the world was threatened with another war. Olive had
strained not to believe him, and they had quarrelled, but oh
how terribly right he had turned out to be. He may not have
had much of an education but he had a nose for the way things
were. In his union he was respected, all his life, looked up to
and respected. The lead-up to the war was all meetings and
rallies and conferences. They had made an anti-war exhibition
and sent it all over England. They'd tried to anticipate what the

outcome of a second world war would be. But they were wrong. Even Arthur was wrong. The truth was so much worse than they had imagined – they who were accused of scaremongering.

In those years before the war they'd hardly seen each other. *Been* together, yes, but hardly had time to notice, caught up in the terrible heady excitement and fear.

And then there was the war, and their separation, and then the time after the war when Arthur lost his fire. Oh he had still dreamt and how she had loved him with his earthy fingers and his dreams.

Between Olive's fingers the rose petal dissolves into flakes. She did love Arthur but . . . if it had only been Arthur that she loved.

If only she had been satisfied. Her memory travels towards darkness now, towards a place where she does not willingly go. She frowns at the pages of the books until the jumping words settle down, and she forces herself to try and make sense of them and of the doings of the Mellstock parish choir among the creaking trees.

*   *   *

Arthur goes out to search for Olive's hat. He takes Kropotkin, who is none the worse for his experience, and together they search in the gutter and under the cars, but they have no luck. It is a grim afternoon now, a proper November afternoon: the paving stones and the slate roofs glint wetly in the light of the watery circle that could be the sun or could be the moon. Drips hang from every twig, every sad privet hedge, and Arthur thinks longingly of his allotment. He fingers the godstone in his pocket.

Olive is getting to be a proper worry nowadays. It is so hard to leave her. It is cruel to leave her for too long, for she loses her bearings. Olive. Desirable Olive. Bright Olive who always knew her mind; who refused to marry him on principle; who campaigned against the war and bravely spent the wartime nights fire-watching or driving ambulances through the blazing streets. His Olive who can't cope now with taking a dog for a short walk. Arthur sniffs. The coldness brings a drop to the end of his nose, but it is sadness that makes his eyes swim. The godstone is warm in his clutch. It will last for ever, stone, unlike flesh, unlike mind, and somehow that is a comfort. Arthur is too in tune with the rising and the dying-away of the seasons, the endless cycle of ends and beginnings, to be in awe of death. But he does love Olive. And it pains him to see her decline.

The hat is nowhere to be seen; some kid must have made off with it. Potkins has had enough. He's decided it's time for his tea and Arthur lets himself be pulled back up the hill. Life is full of sadness and madness, he thinks, and the loss of a cherry hat can break an old woman's heart.

Five

Rodney has turned up for his tea. Selflessly, Nell serves him her piece of smoked haddock on toast with a poached egg, and makes do with an egg herself.

'He used to love this,' Rodney says, tucking in. 'Remember, Mum? They used to have it for Saturday tea, all round the fire. Rodney and Mum and Dad. Trays on their knees. Only time they were ever allowed to eat in front room.'

'I wish you wouldn't sit at the table with your coat on,' sniffs Nell. 'Anyone would think was a transport café to look at you.'

'Sorry.' Rodney stands up and takes off his donkey jacket. Nell whisks it away and hangs it in the cellar head. There is a blast of cold musty air from the cellar before Nell closes the door. 'It's none too warm in here,' Rodney remarks.

'It's quite sufficiently warm, Rodney. You have to expect a bit of a chill this time of year.'

'He had a bit of luck at dogs, last night.'

Nell sniffs. Rodney has a globule of egg-yolk on his chin. Remembering gentlemanly Jim, knowing her own background, it is hard to credit that this lout is really their child. *Lout*. She suffers the word, for if he is a lout, if he is worse, then perhaps it is her own fault. Rodney isn't like most boys . . . men. He needs more supervision, a mother's supervision.

She rinses her hands under the tap and then sits back down opposite him. 'Rodney,' she says. 'You asked me yesterday if you could move back home . . .'

'Yes . . .' Rodney looks at her eagerly, his eyes sharp points behind his thick lenses.

'Well I've reconsidered. You can move back if you wish. But
. . .' she holds up her hand to stall his response, 'there are
conditions.'

'He'll do anything. Anything.'

'I want your hair cut. I want you smartened up. I want to see
you in a job. No more time-wasting, betting, drinking your
money away.'

'Anything.'

Nell controls the twitching of her lips. It is good to please, to
have the power to please someone so. And perhaps it will work
out for the best. Once she's in control, she might make
something of him yet. She pours them each a cup of tea, and
arranges the iced fancies on a paper doily.

'Can he see his room?' Rodney asks. He sinks his teeth into a
yellow fondant diamond and crumbs rain down his front.
Nell's fingers fidget towards the sink, towards the J Cloth, but
she is a model of restraint this evening.

'In a bit,' she says. 'I'll just get the pots out of the way first.'
She moves to the sink and turns on the hot tap.

'He'll just go up and look.' Rodney stands up. 'No need for
you to come.' But Nell dries her hands hastily. She doesn't
want him up there alone. Not yet. That room is her treasure,
her pleasure. He hasn't been in it for years, decades. He hasn't
slept at home since before the trouble and the room is still a
boy's room, her boy's room, nothing to do with this man. She
follows him up the stairs to the small, cold back bedroom. It is
a clean room, a museum of Rodney's childhood. The exhibits
are arranged on the shelves with care, and not a speck of dust
among them. There are cars and boats and trains. There are
aeroplanes constructed from balsa kits, suspended from the
ceiling. There is a Meccano crane, its hook dangling emptily.
There are books: Biggles and Jennings and *Boy's Own*
annuals, fairy tales and poetry.

Reclining on the pillow of Rodney's bed, a narrow bed with

a blue candlewick bedspread, is Mr Wog, Rodney's golliwog, his face as black and beaming as ever. Rodney, wonderingly, picks things up, puts them down all awry. 'You've kept his things. All his things. His Model T Ford, all his Dinkies.'

'It's all here. All as it was when you left. You were only seventeen, and I hoped, we hoped, your dad and I, we just hoped you'd be back. "He'll see sense," he used to say. "Our Rodney's no fool. He knows where he's best off." He so wanted you to take your chances, go to university. Could never believe that you'd throw it all away. "If I'd had his chances," he used to say of an evening when it was all quiet. "Such a bright lad. If only I'd had his chances, what wouldn't I have done? But he'll be back. He knows which side his bread's buttered." But he was wrong, wasn't he? Nearly broke his heart, you did, our Rodney.'

Rodney reaches up and swings one of the aeroplanes. 'His dad put these up for him, with his little tacks and his ladder. And he used to watch them at night. He used to dream of flying.'

'And then when we heard of you next – given you up for dead we had. Ten years! Whatever had we done to deserve that? When we heard of you next it was only because you were in trouble. Only because you needed help. And such trouble! We couldn't understand it. Your dad he just couldn't comprehend. Grey he went, when we got the call. Weren't we good parents to you Rodney? Weren't we?' Nell's voice has risen to a wail and there are spots of pink in her cheeks. Rodney's face too is red. 'Filthy,' she shrieks and Rodney flinches. 'Filthy, filthy, filthy. I've tried Rodney since that day to make things clean, to keep things clean. How any child of Jim's, any child of mine could be so filthy . . .' her voice trails away. Rodney shrugs. He sits down on the bed and picks up Mr Wog.

'And don't sit on that bedspread!' Nell snaps, but Rodney stays put. 'Look around this room,' continues Nell. 'Just you use your eyes and look. Look at the toys and the books. Look at the wallpaper. Cowboys on the wallpaper. And Indians! What more could a lad want, eh? What more could we have done? Ungrateful wretch, that's what you are. And I'm just thankful your dad – God rest his soul – is good and dead to spare him the sight of you now.'

Rodney has moved to the top of the bed. He curls his knees to his chest and hugs Mr Wog tightly to him.

'Look at you!' Nell jeers. 'A grown man! And didn't I tell you not to sit on that bedspread? I've kept it nice without your help all these years . . . Oh and you broke your father's heart. Oh yes you did. And mine too while you were at it. When I think of the times I was up in the night to you, what with your croup and your mumps and your nightmares. Did you ever, ever once, hear a word of complaint? Did you? And there was Daphne parading her perfect Miles in front of us. Just to show us. Just to show us. Why couldn't you have been more like Miles, eh? eh? Weren't we good enough parents for you? Eh? eh?'

'Fuck off,' says Rodney quietly and Nell flinches. He might as well throw a bucket of manure at the walls as use that language in here.

'Don't you use that word to me, Rodney! Not in my home.'

'Oh piss off.' Rodney's voice rises. 'Fuck off you cold old, fucking old bitch!' Spit flies from his mouth as he shouts.

Nell takes a deep breath. Fear and anger fuse in her breast and something like violence flows along her arms and she has to hold them stiff against her sides to stop herself grabbing something and hurling it at him. She is afraid not only of him but of the rage inside her own body, her own controlled body. She calms her breathing using a technique she learnt from breakfast television. Breathe in for ten, out for ten, and so on, until the heartbeat slows, until she regains control. The room is quiet but for her own breathing and a sniffling noise from Rodney.

'I will ask you to leave now,' says Nell.

'Oh no.' Rodney's voice sounds peculiar, a sort of high-pitched, childish whine. He is curled tight around Mr Wog, and his face seems not angry now, but scared. 'He's not leaving now because if he does you'll never have him back. He knows that. He knows you. You're angry with him because he swore, because he's sitting on the precious bedspread. Once you locked him under the stairs for that.'

'I did no such thing!'

'All night. He cried all night.'

'What nonsense!'

'And if he goes now, you'll never have him back.'

'This is my house, and I'm asking you to leave. Son or no son.'

Rodney begins to cry. Nell thinks that he is mad, mad to make up such lies about her. For she did her best, and a boy has to be punished, there has to be discipline. To make such a fuss! He takes off his glasses and scrubs at his eyes with his fists. His eyes are mean and red-rimmed. All the lashes, the lovely long lashes – wasted on a boy they used to say, the women who admired him in his pram – have fallen out. His face crumples horribly into greasy folds as he cries. There is something disgusting about the tears of a grown-up man. A kind of discharge, a diseased overflowing, unwholesome. She never saw his father cry, not once in more than fifty years of marriage. Not Jim.

'I'll leave you to pull yourself together,' says Nell. She is at a loss. The thing to do when people cry is to comfort them, hold them, pat them, dry their tears. When Rodney was a baby she could always make it right, make it all better, just by holding him tight, just by murmuring into his silky hair. But she cannot bring herself to touch this greasy oaf, crumpling and damping the beautiful blue candlewick. She feels the first tendrils of a headache creeping round from the back of her neck towards

her forehead. When they join she will be done in, and bed will
be the only place.

                              *   *   *

In Olive's head there is a song. The words of the song go on
and on, round and round like a merry-go-round. She can
almost feel them spin. The room is full of words tonight. They
spill from the tidy know-it-all lips of the television newscaster
until the room is awash with them. It is the reading that's done
it, the trying to read. Something has been dislodged in her
brain but it is just words, just a welter of unsorted words.
There is no sense in it, no meaning. It is chaos. And the
newscaster keeps on churning them out, words and words and
words about murder and Poland and money and freedom but
the edges are not clear. It is not plain where one thing ends and
another begins and it is no good trying to make sense of it,
there is too much of it, too many words and what with the
raggle-taggle words of the song spinning, it is too much to
bear.

'Artie!' cries Olive, and he, who has been watching her face
as she struggles, gets up immediately.

'I'll switch it off.'

His chair creaks as he settles back down. It is quieter, though
the ghosts of the words hang in the air, fading only gradually.
And the words still rattle inside.

Olive squeezes her eyes shut, squeezes them so hard that the
darkness sparkles. She can feel Arthur looking at her, hear him
sigh. All the bloody years he's been there. All the bloody years.
And where in the world have they gone? It's like a game, a
playground game, suddenly you're out, you've had your turn
and you're out, or the bell goes. All those years since she first
clapped eyes on him, all those years that have just gone, like a
mistake, like a present snatched away from under her nose.

But then it was a life as valid as any other, she must suppose. She worked, he worked, and not just for themselves, they were political, they thought about the state of the world – but the state it's in now is beyond her, and the news is like fragments, puzzle pieces all messed up and no picture to go by and anyhow, who knows if there are any pieces missing? She snorts, impatient with the fancy of it, everything like something else now in her mind, nothing just itself.

She concentrates. She concentrates on remembering Arthur, for that she can remember, every detail as if through a microscope. Arthur with the sun always in his eyes, although of course there could not always have been sun, but still, there he is with the sun in his eyes, blinking and grinning and pushing a lock of his black hair back from his face. And his pullover was green and it had a darn, a bad darn, worse than the hole would have been. And he hadn't had any schooling to speak of and Nell looked down, no doubt, and Jim – though who knows what went on in that one's head – and Arthur always pushed that lock of hair back as he spoke and he might not have had time for school as a lad but he read books, oh yes, and his brain was like fly-paper the way things stuck, every bloody word he read stuck, and he had ideas, he made patterns from the things he read, and he had ideas and he dazzled Olive with his ideas and he dazzled others too, and she used to love to watch him at meetings, she loved to watch other people watching him, watching the light in his eyes, and his brown hand pushing that lock of hair back from his face.

She opens her eyes and there is Arthur on the big chair in the cluttered room. Little shrivelled Arthur. They were the same size once, almost. Funny how she has swelled and he has shrunk about his bones. The first time they met he was handing out leaflets in front of the town hall, leaflets with red borders and swastikas on them, *The Threat of Fascism*, or *Fascism the Threat*, or something like, and afterwards he'd taken her to tea and she'd watched the way his fingers – fingers with earth under the nails, oh he was particular about the house she found later, but always there was earth under his nails – and she watched the way his fingers held the teacup and she'd wanted them on her, all over her, and inside her, and that was that.

'Tea at the Sphere,' she says suddenly, and Arthur blinks at her. 'Cress sandwiches. China tea. Blackcurrant tart and cream.'

Arthur chuckles. 'So that's it. I was wondering where you'd got to.'

'And didn't I think you were flush!'

'I lived on bread and dripping for a week! Over fifty bally years ago that were Ollie. Over half a century. Can you believe it?'

'I can believe it.' The memory is clear, like a straight path through a wood, and the trees move back from the path and Olive can remember the song now. Her voice rises in a croaking song. The words slide from her head, easy now, sensible now. It is her grandmother's song:

What care I now for my goosefeather bed,
With the sheets turned down so bravely oh?
Tonight I will sleep in a cold open field.
Along with the raggle-taggle gypsies oh.

Olive closes her eyes, relieved at this feat of memory, stretching it back now, as far back as there is: the black dress of her grandmother and her blue-veined hands stroking, stroking Olive's hair in time with her song. And now Olive is as old, at least as old, as her grandmother was then.

'And they've been grand years,' says Arthur.

'And I was beautiful.'

'As beautiful as any that's lived.'

'And now I'm old.' Olive opens her eyes and glares at him,

suddenly fierce. It is all right remembering scraps, being grateful for scraps, but she is angry, angry that she can't live for ever, that gradually it's fading away. 'Not beautiful now. An old burden now. A fat old bugger of a burden who pees herself and . . .'

'No! I won't have you talking like that.'

Olive flings the sweet tin away from her and it crashes against the gas fire, causing Mao to leap up and dart behind Arthur's chair.

'Now, now,' Arthur says.

'And I want my hat!' Olive shouts. 'Want it back, my cherry hat!' For it is not fair. Yes all right she will die, just like her grandmother, just like . . . she will not think of him now. All right, she knows it must be so. She will follow them into death – but why can't it be sudden? Why must it all peel away so terribly gradually: beauty, memory, dignity? Why could she not even keep the hat?

'It's gone, me duck, you know it's gone. We can always get you another,' soothes Arthur, but Olive will not be soothed. How can Arthur accept it so easily? For he is grown old too. His face is shrunken like a little brown monkey's and his brows hang down over his watery eyes. He is a meek old man, grown tame with the years, driving Olive mad with his patience.

'There's chocolate from next door,' Arthur tries. 'They said you asked for it.'

'Oh bugger the chocolate. Think you can shut me up. Stuff me full of sweets.'

'Ollie . . .'

'I'm off to bed.' She struggles on to all fours and pulls herself up, shrugging off Arthur's attempts to help. 'Think I need you. Think I can't cope,' she mutters. She stands up and the pain in her back is fierce and Arthur is there, just too close and she cannot stand it and she hits out. Her arm is heavy and she hurts him, she can feel from the thud, the way it catches his shoulder, the way he gasps. And he leaves the room, for he would never hit Olive, not in a million years, and though she meant to hurt him and is partly satisfied by the solidity of the blow, she is also sorry. He's a poor old bugger. They are poor old buggers together. She hears the back door bang and supposes that he has gone to Potkins for solace. Mao puts his head round the corner of the chair, regards her with his cold blue blink. She shuffles to the bottom of the stairs and begins her slow ascent. When Arthur comes back she will apologise. She is not proud. And then, perhaps, she *will* have a bit of that chocolate.

*   *   *

Nell sits on a chair in the cold kitchen. Her legs are stiff, knees clamped tight together, and she picks at one fingernail with another. The only sound is the dry clicking she makes — like a clock counting off the seconds.

The floor is damp for it has just been mopped and there is a clean smell, a germ-killing smell in the air. The dish-mop and the J Cloths are soaking in bleach. The head of the floor-mop is wrung into a tight white wisp and stands upright, airing. The bucket is upside-down on a page from the *Mail* to ensure that it is bone-dry inside. For Nell has seen, in her Sunday supplement, the things that will live and breed in a dirty house. She has seen them magnified many thousand times into monsters with scales and claws, with a look of blank malevolence in their bulging eyes. Every crevice offers a home to living, crawling filth. A teaspoonful of dirt collected from around the house may contain hundreds of millions of miniscule monsters, more than there are people in the world. Nell must try not to think of that fact. Ever since Rodney's disgrace she has waged war on the filth, but there will always be more. Even on herself, on her skin, within her mouth, her nose, under her fingernails and in her gut they breed, the creatures. When she bathes, she bathes in Dettol. She breathes in and screws shut her mouth and her eyes, and pinches her nostrils together and she immerses herself in the hot disinfectant. It bubbles fiercely against her ear-drums, it stings her in the most tender places but at least it helps. At least it floats away the surface dirt.

Now she sits in her kitchen and at least the floor is clean. Nell shivers. The colder it is in a house, the less chance that the pests will thrive, will mate, will squirt out their disgusting eggs and spawn. Nell shivers again. She is tired. It is well past bed-time. Jim will be wondering where she's got to. But how can she go to bed now? Upstairs there is a man in her little boy's bed, a man who might as well be a stranger. He has crumpled the candlewick and rumpled the sheets. Lice are most likely crawling from his hair, tumbling onto the pillow where her boy's head used to rest in innocent sleep.

The claws around Nell's head tighten. She has taken tablets and she has mopped the floor to try and work away the tension, to keep control, but still the claws tighten. She sees the headache as a beast with a face, a sticky crab or spider with the vacuous eyes of a magnified flea. It clings tighter and she scrubs frantically at her head, but what can she do? How can she ever sleep with that creature in the house?

*　*　*

Arthur stands out the back looking at the city lights. Car lamps flow along a distant road like bright beads on a string. Kropotkin snuffles round his feet. Arthur sighs and turns his back on the endless busyness of the city. He looks up at the backs of the houses. Their own is in darkness except for the kitchen light which he will soon switch off before bed. But he cannot go to bed until he is calm. Arthur is gentle, peaceful. He has never hit a person in his life, apart from the odd playground scuffle as a lad. He has never hurt a person. He would not fight in the war because of his conviction that physical force is wrong, and he is damned if he is going to go against all his principles now and slap Olive hard round the face, which is what he itches to do. Not that he doesn't love her, oh no, not that he doesn't adore her. But she drives him crazy sometimes with the way she changes, the way she blows hot and cold, the way she remembers and the way she forgets.

All the lights are on next door by the look of it. Feckless – but all the same it does look warm like that, all the bright rectangles, not even a curtain drawn. And even in Nell's house there is an upstairs light on. The back-bedroom light. Odd. That is, surely that is, the boy's bedroom. Rodney's. Perhaps Nell is in there, remembering. Jim told him how she kept his room like a shrine, everything in place so neat, so clean. A child's bedroom complete with everything but a flesh-and-blood child. Whatever must it be like to have a child, a living child? Arthur remembers the unbearable softness of a new-born head. He remembers the tiny hands, pink daisies of hands, opening and closing on his calloused thumb. He remembers Olive with her creamy breasts spilling from her scarlet nightdress, with her face and her hair glowing in the lamp-light. He blinks and sniffs. There was never the time to get used to it, used to having a child in the house. The lad never even had a room of his own, he slept beside their bed so that Olive could reach out to him, easy in the night. They never mention him. Of course, they both remember, but they never mention his name. Does she dream, Arthur wonders, as he frequently does, of the lad – grown-up as he now would be – when she's lost in the blessed deepness of her sleep?

He shakes the scales of sadness from him. Kropotkin turns eagerly towards the gate, turns back to Arthur and looks up at him, his head cocked comically in a question. Arthur chuckles. 'All right, old lad,' he says and reaches down to attach the lead to the dog's collar.

* * *

Nell holds her breath. She pushes open the door of Rodney's room, and peers in. He is curled on his side with his face to the wall. He is on top of the covers still, but at least he has taken off his shoes. She cannot see his face, but she can hear a suckling sound. He is sucking his thumb. The measures she went to to stop that dirty habit! Mustard on his thumb, a glove, even his hands tied together, and now he lies there, middle-aged man that he is, curled up like some grotesque infant, and still he sucks his thumb.

She switches off the light and closes the door quietly. If only there was a bolt. If only she could lock him in . . . She uses the lavatory and scrubs it and pours bleach down it and then she washes. She listens outside Rodney's door on her way back to her bedroom — but it is all quiet. She goes into her own room and closes the door firmly. She pushes the chair across the floor and jams it under the door-handle.

'What are you afraid of?' asks Jim.

'You didn't hear what he said to me. Talk about language!'

'I did hear, Nell. He was upset.'

'*He* was upset!' She pulls her nightdress on over the top of her clothes and then turns away from him and fumbles her clothes off underneath.

'He's been ill, remember, Nell. Make allowances. Perhaps he is still . . . suffering in his mind.'

'Well he's never got it from my side. There was never any madness on my side.'

'You know he'd never hurt you. He loves you. He loves you too much. He wouldn't harm a hair on your head. All he ever wanted was to please you.'

'Funny way he had of showing it!'

'You made it too hard for him. He could never match up . . .

little wonder he gave up trying . . . If you'd only let the boy grow up, Nell, but you had to try and hold him back . . .'

'Oh! So that's the way the land lies. My fault. All my fault. I see!'

'No I didn't mean . . .' begins Jim, but it is too late. She knocks him smartly down onto his front, before getting into bed. The sheets are cool and smooth and tight as she eases herself between them, causing as little disturbance as possible. It is good to lie down, and the cold pillow absorbs some of the throbbing of her head as she lies stiffly, her ears tuned to Rodney's room.

It is not easy to be a mother, she thinks, and it occurs to her that she never thinks of her own mother. It's funny how she never remembers her, for she must have been there. If there was a family outing there would be Mother and Father and Eleanor and Edwin, and sometimes Olive or one of Edwin's friends. She remembers a Sunday outing, a warm day, May or June. They had gone out, just the four of them, grand and swanky in Father's new motor car, sweeping proudly through the streets. Nell can still recall the rush of the warm polleny air against her face, the way it played with her wonderful sausagey ringlets. They had picnicked in a hollow near the shallow plashy river, in a place where the rocks were huge and warm and flat. Father had been back from the war only a few months and still seemed strange and distant, tall and handsome and still rather brown from the Turkish sun. And Nell so wanted to impress him. How she tried! After the sandwiches and the cold chicken and the cake, Edwin had taken off his shoes and stockings and Father had cheered as he leapt from rock to rock. 'Bravo!' he shouted and clapped his hands. And to Nell it seemed an awful fuss to make for it was not far to jump and the stones were so flat and safe. Nell picked Father some flowers, but there was nothing much to pick, only tiny insipid things, and it was a miserable spiky little posy she presented him with, and he hardly even looked. He kept his eyes on Edwin's antics. Edwin had wet feet now, and sprang from rock to rock leaving the neat prints of his feet behind him, and Nell couldn't bear it. It wasn't as if he was doing anything clever; she could do just as well.

She crept down behind a crease in the ground and unlaced her tight black boots and peeled off her stockings and then she jumped out. 'Look at me!' she cried. 'Look, Father, watch *me*, watch *me*!' and she leapt from one rock to another and another, getting faster and faster, and dazzling Father, she expected, with her agility, until she tripped and fell face-downwards into the water. She thought for a moment that she was dead, the silence that followed her splash was so complete. And then she thought that Father would scoop her up in his great soldier's arms and save her. But no. There was just Edwin prancing about and laughing and calling her a nincompoop. She had to struggle up herself to face a very cold look from Father and some talk of ladylike behaviour. And then there was the drive home with the wind, cold now, blowing in her face and her teeth chattering and the sopping muslin of her dress clinging to her and her ringlets all dropped out, and no one taking a bit of notice, except Edwin pulling faces and folding his lip up over his nose in a way that she could never manage. She was put to bed with a hot-water bottle when they got home, and the incident was never mentioned again.

Six

Wolfe stands beside Buffy at the kitchen table. They have the fireworks spread out before them. 'This is *my* rocket,' says Wolfe.

'Who said? It's the biggest and you're the smallest. You can have this one.' Buffy shoves an inferior rocket towards him.

'Don't want that one.'

'You can have the sparklers. Well most of the sparklers. You can have Vesuvius.'

Wolfe pauses, considering. He likes the cone shape of the volcano, with its blue touchpaper poking from the top, already like a little flame. 'And Traffic Lights?' he bargains.

Petra comes into the kitchen in her nightdress. 'We're all going to see all of them,' she points out, 'so what does it matter?' Wolfe scowls at her. Grown-ups can be so stupid sometimes. It is fun to look at the fireworks and to say their names, and to know that some of them are yours. And *of course* they will all see all of them. That isn't the point.

'The Catherine wheel's like an ammonite,' he says.

' 'Snot,' says Buffy.

'Like that ammonite I used to have, remember Mum? At the Longhouse. I wish I'd brought it with me now.'

Petra slices bread and switches on the grill. 'Clear those off the table,' she says. 'I'm having breakfast. Anyone else want any toast?'

'Fireworks are dangerous,' Wolfe says. 'School says we should go to the park and watch the musical ones.'

'Municipal,' corrects Buffy. 'Bloody neurotic if you ask me.'

'They're quite safe if you're careful,' Petra says. 'Better say now if you want some toast.'

'I'm slimming,' says Buffy.

'I'm having Weetabix.' Wolfe packs the fireworks carefully back into their box. His hands feel greasy from the fine leaking of gunpowder. Tomorrow is the day. It almost seems a shame to set them off. Lovely things. But it is exciting. It will be exciting. A party, with Arthur and the old ladies and Tom. 'I'm going out with Tom today, aren't I Mum?'

Petra winces. 'Oh, I don't know.'

'But he said,' Wolfe wails.

'I know love, but you know what Tom is. Something came up and he had to go off last night to see someone in Leeds. He might be back but . . .' she trails off, dips the tip of her knife in the Marmite jar. Wolfe watches the neat way she spreads so that every speck of toast is covered.

'Bloody liar he is,' he says.

'Wolfe! Don't you start! He's not a liar, he's just forgetful. But he will take you. Another day. I promise. And what do you mean, you're slimming?' Petra switches her attention to Buffy.

Wolfe sighs. It's always the same. He doesn't know why he bothers to believe Tom. They always tell you Don't lie, don't make promises you can't keep, grown-ups do, but they do it themselves, Tom does specially but they all do it sometimes, even Petra.

Bobby comes down, scowling. 'Did you hear that effing dog next door? Wants putting down.' He takes a mug off the draining board and slams it down.

'Make me a cup of tea, love,' says Petra through a mouthful of toast.

'I was having coffee . . . oh all right.'

'We'd better go out fetching wood for the bonfire,' says Buffy.

'There's more important things than that,' Bobby says.

'Such as?'

'Penny for the bleeding guy!'

'Bobby, really! Do you have to swear every other word?' mutters Petra.

'Then we can buy *more* fireworks, proper bangers and stuff, instead of these farty Snowflakes and Starbursts.'

'Spoilt brat,' complains Petra. 'When I was thirteen I was grateful for what I was given. I'd have had a clipped ear and been locked in my bedroom for a week if I'd gone on like you.'

'Bring on the violins. Here's your tea.' Bobby puts a mug down in front of Petra.

'Thanks. And I don't know about penny for the guy. Remember trick-or-treating? You all came back scared stiff.'

'Did not. And we won't have Wolfe with us this time.' Wolfe sticks out his tongue but he doesn't care. He doesn't want to stand about all day. He'd rather get on with the fire. He'd rather have the box of fireworks all to himself to play with.

'I don't like you begging,' Petra insists, but it is obvious that her heart isn't in it.

'Go on, Mum. I've got to buy Nothing a litter tray. She did it all over my homework last night.'

'Told you it was a load of crap,' says Bobby.

'Told you you'd regret keeping it,' Petra adds.

'Her, and I *don't*.'

'Where is it anyway?'

'There.' Buffy points to Tom's tennis shoe which lies in the middle of the floor. It is filled with a black shape, soft as a shadow.

'That's the last place I'd choose to sleep!' Petra smiles wearily at them. 'Oh all right then, but be sensible. And I expect you to spend any money you make on buying what you need for Nothing. Understand? And don't go hassling people.'

'Come on Buff, let's get on with the guy,' Bobby says. 'Got anything else we can dress it in, Mum?'

'Not really. Nothing I don't want. Haven't you got anything you don't want?'

'We'll have a look.' Bobby and Buffy go off upstairs and Wolfe helps himself to some Weetabix.

'Last day of the holiday,' he says miserably. 'Only Saturday and Sunday and then school. I hate that school, Mum.'

'Oh dear . . .'

'I wish we could go home.'

'This is . . .'

'It's not, not to me. The Longhouse is home to me.'

Petra sighs. She puts her hand on the top of her belly. 'Oooh,' she says. Wolfe looks and sees a little knobbly shape rising and falling, right through Petra's nightdress. It makes him feel funny. Fascinated and queasy at the same time.

'Want to feel?' Petra asks. Wolfe doesn't really, but he puts out his hand and waits and almost takes his hand away for he can't feel anything, and then suddenly there is a slithery jab and he jumps back surprised.

'What was that?'

'A knee, I think,' she says. There is something horrible about it, a wet fishy baby thing crammed in there, something rude and scary. Petra puts her arm round him. 'Don't look like that! What are you planning to do today?'

Wolfe shrugs. He looks over Petra's shoulder and he sees the top of a cloth cap outside the window. 'It's Arthur!' he cries, as Arthur knocks on the door. Wolfe rushes to open it. 'Hello Arthur,' he says. 'Come in.'

'I don't know . . .' says Arthur, putting his head round the door. He catches sight of Petra in her nightdress. 'Sorry,' he says, retreating hastily.

'It's all right,' calls Petra. 'I'm quite decent, I think. Anyway I'm past caring.'

'I'm just asking if lad wants to walk up allotment with me and dog.' Potkins yaps, and tries to pull Arthur in.

'Yes please,' breathes Wolfe.

'Fine. He's at a bit of a loose end, aren't you love?' Petra sips her tea. Wolfe wishes she was dressed. Her belly looks disgusting with her nightdress stretched so tight across it that her belly button shows, sticking out like a little knob. However, Arthur remains discreetly out of sight.

'I'll just get my shoes on,' Wolfe says. Arthur beams at him. 'Wait there.'

'Better put your wellies on,' advises Petra.

'I'll just shut door or dog'll be in,' Arthur says. He reaches his hand in and shuts himself out.

'That's good, isn't it Wolfie?' Petra says. 'I think I might take my cup of tea up to bed for half an hour. Don't be a nuisance, will you?' Wolfe, struggling into his boots, wobbles on one foot and frowns at her.

'Course not,' he says.

*　*　*

Nell wakes with a start. It is light, and therefore late. She suspects she's been snoring, and she has certainly been dreaming. She tries to grasp the shreds of the dream but they will not be grasped. They dissolve into the light, and perhaps it is just as well. She does not think that it was a cheerful dream. She runs through her plans for the day: it's Friday so the paintwork wants doing. It's hard on her knees, Friday, for she has to go round all the skirtings with disinfectant and then there are the door- and window-frames. A hard day, but she likes to be spick and span for the weekend. Then there is the shopping, that must wait till after lunch. She's lucky if she gets her nap on Fridays. The filthy hat still sits on top of the wardrobe. Whatever was she thinking of, bringing it home? She'll get shot of it today, sling it across the gardens for them to find – that will puzzle them – or else bin it.

She smiles and stretches, prepares to get up – and then she hears a crash downstairs. She gasps, feels cold fear sweep over her like a wave. And then she remembers: Rodney is here. The bright prospect of a clean and busy day dims, and she groans. She notices Jim lying on his face and remembers the quarrel. You'd think death would put a stop to all that. She sits up and does a few of her breaths to steady her nerves and then she stands him up.

'Don't start,' she warns.

'No,' he says, 'only remember, Nell. Our son. Be fair to him, for my sake.'

'Saint Jim,' she scoffs. She goes to the bathroom to dress, uses the lavatory furtively. She likes privacy, does Nell. Downstairs, the kettle is whistling, and so is Rodney.

'Morning,' he says. 'Sleep well?'

'Do I ever?' she answers, although in fact it is the best night's sleep she's had in years.

'What's for breakfast? He's mashing tea.'

'I always have All-Bran and a spot of toast,' says Nell. 'I suppose I could do you an egg.'

'With Marmite soldiers? He always loved Marmite soldiers.'

'He – you – can cut your own soldiers, though really at your age . . . but a soft-boiled egg, yes. Perhaps I'll join you.' Nell fills a pan and puts it on to boil. The kitchen smells of Rodney. 'You get your hands washed and get sat down,' she says.

'He's sorry,' Rodney says, 'about last night.'

Nell takes two stainless-steel egg-cups from the kitchen cupboard and gives them a wipe-round. 'We'll say no more for now,' she replies. 'But I want you to stop this "he" business. I find it unnerving. You are you.'

Rodney looks down. 'You mean his language.'

'No, I mean . . .' but Rodney looks at her blankly, stupidly, and she breaks off. The greasy sheen of his glasses reminds her for a split second of the eyes of the beast, germ eyes, and she looks away, swallows. 'Never mind.'

She lowers two eggs carefully into the gently bubbling water and tips up the egg timer. It was a present from Jim, brought back from a business trip somewhere or other. Fine white sand flows through glass held between porcelain hands. Peculiar really. She feels a nervous creeping in her diaphragm. 'We'll not go into details about your behaviour,' she says, watching the steam rise from the water; tiny bubbles appear on the shells, the eggs stir with the water's movement. 'Suffice it to say that it will not do. If you want to stay here, Rodney, if you want to live here, you must behave. As you very well know. Behave.'

'He will.'

'Well make sure he does.' Nell flinches. 'You do.'

Nell lays the table: plates, knives, spoons, cups and saucers, and as she arranges them she is whisked back to breakfast-times long ago, before the trouble, before the filth, when Rodney was her sweet schoolboy, important in his uniform. All his life ahead of him, and what hopes didn't she have for him? She struggles to think positive, as they recommend these days, in the magazines. He is not perfect, even the most doting mother in the world couldn't pretend that. He is very far from perfect. But he is *here*, and he isn't a bad son as sons go. He visits her, and that is fine, that is in her control. It is the thought of him living here that worries her.

She puts Rodney's egg in front of him and sits down opposite. He slices the top off his egg and dips a bread finger deep into the yolk and she watches the stream of sticky yellow overflow and run down the side of the shell and the egg-cup.

'Perfect,' Rodney says. He chews for a moment and then smiles across at Nell. 'You always gave him an egg for his breakfast, a proper start, you used to say. And here he is, back home again. Like the old days.'

'Behaviour includes not speaking with your mouth full,' Nell snaps, and then feels sorry. 'But we'll say no more for now. I don't expect they go in for proper behaviour, the sort of company you've been keeping. Just do your best.'

'He'll fetch his stuff this morning.'

'Hold your horses, Rodney. We can give it a week or two . . .'

'But he's here now. He's slept here.'

Nell pours out the tea. 'Yes, but,' but quick as she is she cannot think of a reason to put him off. Not a reason she can admit to Rodney.

Rodney slurps. 'He *can* stay then?'

'Behaviour includes these things, Rodney: no foul language, no elbows on the table, no talking with your mouth full *or* eating with your mouth open. It means no sitting on the bedspread. It means leaving the lavatory *as you would wish to find it* . . .'

'All right –'

'And no interrupting.'

'I'll fetch my things this morning.'

Nell hesitates. Perhaps it is as well to jump in at the deep end. She taps the top of her egg delicately with her teaspoon, as if politely requesting admittance. She thinks of Jim upstairs, big-hearted Jim, powerless in his frame. 'Oh all right,' she says. 'Why I'm so soft I don't know. You can scarcely claim to deserve it. But come back via the barber's, understand. Short back and sides before you re-enter this house.'

Rodney grins. Nell dips her teaspoon in the egg-yolk. It is a bright splashy yellow, and it is *not* just right, Jim's timer has failed her, there are clinging traces of clear gelatinous white. Eggs have been in the news lately, she remembers, featured as unclean. Nell, up to now, has taken no notice. An egg is an egg as far as she's concerned, perfectly sealed into its shell, untouched by human hand. If you can't trust an egg what can you trust? Propaganda, she took it for. Trying to blame the government for the centre of an egg! You might as well blame it for the stars. But all the same, she puts down her spoon. She'd have done better to stick with her All-Bran after all.

* * *

'There,' breathes Arthur proudly. Arthur and Wolfe stand at the top of the allotments looking down towards the river and the park.

'It's beautiful,' says Wolfe but that is not what he means, he means more than that but doesn't have the words. It is more than beautiful. The morning is mild and a pale sun shines across the plots of land, glinting on the bare twigs of the fruit bushes and the roofs of the little sheds. Everything is still. Leaves hang damply or flop crumpled on the ground, onion flowers glow like little planets. Nothing moves. Even the one figure on the allotment, an old man bent over his spade, is motionless, like a man in a painting. The smell is green and brown and cool and rich. In a rush of homesickness Wolfe thinks of the Longhouse garden.

'Yes,' agrees Arthur. 'It's grand. Can you guess which is mine?'

Wolfe stands on tiptoe to see better and looks critically at the plots. Arthur's will be the best, he knows that much. He screws his nose up in concentration and feels Arthur smile down at him.

'I'll give you a clue, it's lower down,' he says.

'That one,' decides Wolfe suddenly, pointing at a newly dug patch, neatly marked out with twigs.

'I'll be blowed!' laughs Arthur. 'Got it in one! How did you know?'

Wolfe is relieved. 'Not sure, it just sort of . . . looks like you, I s'pose.'

Arthur's shoulders rise as he chuckles. He takes Wolfe's hand

and squeezes it in his own, which feels as hard as leather. 'Want to take a closer look?'

'Course I do.'

'Over here then,' Arthur points to a low stile. Wolfe scrambles over, and Arthur struggles with Potkins who tangles round his legs in his eagerness to follow. They walk down a steep narrow path, slippery with stones and damp grass. Birds rustle in the thorn hedges. Just for a moment Wolfe forgets the town, feels that he's back in the country again.

'Here we are.' The path opens out onto the lower allotments where the sudden sound of the river tumbling over its stones is a surprise. 'All right, Fred?' Arthur calls to the old man, who has come alive and is pulling things out of the ground.

'Considering,' the man replies.

Arthur walks across one allotment that looks as if it's just been left to go wild, and across a grass boundary to his own. He shows Wolfe all his plants and his gooseberry bushes; he shows him his seedbed and his cold-frame and his water-butt. He unlocks his shed and Wolfe steps inside, breathing in the delicious smell of dry earth and string. He looks at Arthur's tools, spades and forks and rakes and hoes. They are so old that the wooden handles are pitted and worn like things in a museum. There is a very old lawn-mower and piles of flowerpots, and panes of glass leaning against the wall, there are old tins full of bits and bobs on the shelf, and bundles of green netting hanging from hooks. There is a rickety folding chair. It is clean and neat and orderly and Wolfe loves it.

'When I'm grown-up I'm going to have an allotment,' he declares. 'And I'm going to have a shed just like yours. 'Zactly the same.'

'I don't doubt it, lad,' says Arthur.

'And if we go back I'm going to help in the proper garden. They usually give kids little gardens of their own but they're too small to grow much in. There was only really room for radishes.'

'Go back?'

'I want to go back to our old house. Like I told you, the Longhouse it's called and it's a commune and it had a great garden.'

'A commune eh?'

'Yes, lots of people and all that.' Wolfe strokes the handle of Arthur's fork covetously.

'And what made you move away?'

'Love,' says Wolfe wearily. 'Mum fell in love but I think it was a bit of a mistake really.' Arthur's lips twitch.

'Oh?'

'Well Tom's un . . . un something or other. He never does what he says.'

'Unreliable?'

'Yes. Like he said he'd take me out today and then he went away. That's another thing, he's always going away.'

'Well,' says Arthur cautiously. 'Sometimes folk can't help going away – but you're always welcome to come here with me. Potkins!' The dog makes a sudden lunge at a thrush, which is busy battering a snail upon a stone. Wolfe suddenly notices how small Arthur is for a grown-up man, how tiny he is inside his clothes. His legs inside his baggy brown trousers seem no thicker than the bean-sticks neatly bundled in the corner of the shed. He looks down at his own stout legs in their too-small jeans.

'Thanks,' he says. 'Do you want to come to our bonfire party?'

'Oh I don't think . . .'

'Mum said. She's going to ask. And I've got to ask you if you've got any wood for our fire.'

Arthur gathers together a pile of stuff to be burnt, including some good thick wood from an old window-frame. 'That lot'll burn like the clappers,' he says. 'But we'll never fetch it back.'

'That's OK,' Wolfe says. 'Tom can come and collect it in the car.'

'That's all right then.'

'And you will come to our party,' begs Wolfe. 'Please. It won't be much of a party if no one comes.'

Arthur laughs. 'I'll see what I can do,' he promises. 'We'd better get off now.' Wolfe looks regretfully around. It is so lovely here, a bit like the Longhouse garden, but different because it's all broken up into separate bits. And Arthur is his first new friend, even if he is old.

'Next time I'll help you dig shall I?' he says.

'There's nowt like a bit of help,' Arthur says agreeably. Wolfe stands on the grass boundary waiting for Arthur to lock his shed.

'Did you plant this grass?' he asks.

'No,' Arthur replies. He puts his keys in his pocket. 'Come on Potty.' He tugs Kropotkin to his feet. 'No, my mate Jim turfed that over. There were a bomb in war. God only knows the point of bombing allotments! Anyhow, it landed just there, where you're stood now, and wrecked the lot. I was away at time and Jim sorted out mess. This here were his allotment. He's passed on now but he'd turn in his grave if he could see the state it's in now.'

Arthur turns round and smiles at Wolfe. 'Now let's be off.'

Seven

Wolfe looks uneasily at the guy, who lolls in the corner of Bobby and Buffy's room. He is a clumsy guy, hasty, his face scrawled on a paper bag, his body lumpy. A pair of Petra's tights knobbly as Christmas stockings tail off into limply trailing feet. He is a guy with a funny lopsided face, an almost-smile. A nice guy. Wolfe feels sorry already that he has to burn.

'It won't hurt,' he whispers. He reaches out his hand and dares to touch the guy lightly on the corner of his paper head. 'You're not real, so it can't.' And then he flees downstairs as the screwed-up paper stuffing shifts and crackles.

'Aren't you going to help me with this toffee?' asks Petra. She is searching in the kitchen cupboard. 'I'm sure I've got some black treacle somewhere.'

'Course,' says Wolfe. 'What shall I do first?'

'I'll call you when I'm ready.' Petra frowns at him. 'Have you seen it? I know we've got a tin. Otherwise *someone* will have to run down to the shop.' She looks out of the window at Bobby and Buffy who are building the fire. 'Why don't you help Bob and Buff for now. I'll call you when I'm ready.'

Bobby and Buffy are arranging the wood into a wigwam shape. 'This is brilliant,' Buffy says, 'this wood from next door.'

'I got that,' Wolfe reminds them. They ignore him.

'We need more though, little sticks and stuff, kindling,' Bobby says.

'Where shall we get that from?'

'The park?'

'We haven't got time to go faffing about picking up twigs,'

94

Bobby says. 'We've got to get some more money. We might get more today since it's actually the day.'

'We need to make the guy a bit better,' Buffy says. 'I think that was the trouble before. It doesn't look as if we've taken much time over it.'

'We could ask that side if she's got anything to burn.' Bobby nods at Nell's house. 'Then we could do the guy up a bit and get going.'

'You ask.'

'Will you ask, Wolfe?' Buffy asks him, giving him her brilliant smile.

'No, I'm helping Mum with the toffee,' Wolfe says. He goes back into the kitchen. Petra is kneeling on the floor with her head under the sink. She gives a little muffled cry. 'Here it is! I knew I'd seen it somewhere odd.' She emerges with the sticky tin, her face red from the effort of searching.

'Are you all right?' Wolfe asks. 'Only you look a bit funny.'

'I'm fine.' Petra struggles to her feet. 'In fact I feel very well today. Let's get this toffee made, then I'm going to clean out that cupboard – it's revolting under there, all damp and full of God knows what.'

'What shall I do then?' Wolfe loves cooking. He loves the pots and pans and wooden spoons and he loves the warm smell you get when the things melt together in the pan, especially sweet things.

'Weigh some brown sugar,' Petra says. 'A pound.'

'We do kilograms at school.'

'I don't. Nor do my scales. A pound.'

Wolfe spoons the sugar carefully into the shallow dish of the scales, watching the needle wobble and flicker towards the one-pound mark. It is like dark damp sand, stuck together in hard lumps at the bottom of the bag. He pops a lump in his mouth and it melts on his tongue in a sweet sandy pool.

'Teeth,' warns Petra, and then she laughs and takes a lump herself.

'A pound,' announces Wolfe when the needle on the scales has arrived at the mark. 'Now what?'

'Tip it in the pan. Then you want . . .' Petra squints at a soft old bit of paper, 'two ounces of butter – it'll have to be marge – and four of water. And then two tablespoons of treacle. OK? Just bung it all in the pan. This is my mum's recipe you know.'

'My granny?'

'Would have been. We always had Bonfire toffee.'

'Why did she die?' Wolfe prizes the lid off the treacle tin with a knife.

'Careful. She had a bad heart, I told you before. Now try not to dribble it everywhere.'

'I haven't got a granny or a grandad or a dad,' Wolfe grumbles, pushing the spoon into the stiff black treacle. It is like tar. It smells a bit like tar on the road on a hot day, and it trails from the spoon in sticky ropes as he tries to tip it into the pan.

'No, but you've got me. And Bob and Buff and this . . .' She pats her tummy. 'You're better off than lots of children. Watch what you're doing with that.' Wolfe licks his treacly fingers which taste dark and sweet, like sugary blood. The handle of the spoon is sticky and treacle crawls down the sides of the tin.

'Mum . . .' he says, looking at her helplessly, and she sighs and whips the spoon away from him and twists it round and conjures the second spoonful into the pan.

'Right. I'll put this chair in front of the cooker so that you can stir it yourself. And I'll grease the tin ready for you.' Wolfe climbs up and Petra lights the gas under the saucepan. 'Now, keep stirring until the margarine melts and then the sugar dissolves. It takes ages, but you must keep stirring.'

'Mum!' cries Buffy suddenly bursting in through the door. 'That side hasn't got any wood but look! She's given us a hat for the guy. Isn't it great?'

'Except it's a girl's hat,' complains Bobby.

'So? Why can't it be a girl guy? Sexist,' retorts Buffy.

'Because it was a man, dickhead.'

'Bobby, please,' Petra says frowning at him. 'Let's see.' She holds out her hand for the hat. She turns it round in her hands, a greedy expression on her face. It is an old black straw hat with cherries on the brim that look good enough to eat.

'Do you know, I'm sure I've seen this before,' she says. 'I wonder where. It's a good hat.' She puts it on her head, tilted to one side. 'What do you think?' she asks Buffy. Buffy shrugs. 'It seems a terrible shame to burn it.'

'Well you're not having it,' says Buffy, snatching it from her head.

'No, let's have another look,' Petra fingers the cherries almost as if she is hungry. 'It's certainly too good to burn. Where's Nothing?'

'Dunno. Asleep upstairs I think.'

'I'll give you a fiver to buy the stuff you need for Nothing, if you give me the hat.'

'*Sell* you the hat,' Buffy says with narrowed eyes.

'Oh . . . if you like.'

'Is this done?' Wolfe asks.

Petra glances into the pan. 'Not yet. It's got to boil.'

'Half each,' Bobby says. 'She gave it to both of us.'

'We'll sell you the hat *after* we've done penny for the guy,' decides Buffy. 'And we want six quid, that's three each.'

'No,' says Petra.

'All right, we'll burn it then.'

'Oh all right.' Petra smiles ruefully and hands the hat back to Buffy, and she and Bobby thunder triumphantly upstairs to renovate the guy. 'That sister of yours . . .' she grumbles, but her voice is admiring.

Black bubbles begin to rise in the pan, as if there are

creatures in there trying to heave themselves out of the
stickiness. 'Look Mum,' Wolfe says.

'Boiling point. Now we'll leave it for a minute and then test
it,' Petra says. 'That's the difficult bit.' She stops for a moment,
her hand on her side, a surprised look on her face. 'Ooooh,' she
breathes.

'Are you all right?' says Wolfe, worried. 'You're not having
the baby now are you?'

'Don't be silly.'

'Come on then, let's test it,' he says, relieved. They don't
want the baby arriving right in the middle of the toffee-
making, after all. Petra fills an old marmalade jar with water.
'What you have to do,' she says, 'is this.' She lifts the wooden
spoon from the pan and lets a few drops of the toffee mixture
fall into the water. It dissolves in a dirty cloud. She tips it out
into the sink and fills the jar with clean water. 'Not ready.
When you do that and it goes into a firm lump, it's done. All
right? I'm going to make a start on the cupboard. Call me
when it's ready and I'll help you tip it into the tin.'

'Look!' say Bobby and Buffy proudly. 'Good innit?' They
carry the guy into the kitchen, holding an arm each, and it does
look better – and much more real. It wears the hat at a cheeky
angle, pulled down over one eye, and under the hat it has black
woollen hair hanging down. They have given it red lips, open
lips. It looks as if it is about to speak. It looks as if it wants to
speak to Wolfe and, say, 'Help me.' Wolfe looks away.

'Amazing!' says Petra, coming out from under the sink.
'Where did the wool come from?'

'Come on then,' Bobby says. 'See you.'

'Found it,' Buffy says, pulling on her coat. 'See you later.'

''Bye,' say Petra and Wolfe together.

'Poor guy,' Wolfe says when they've gone.

'Silly!' Petra pulls herself to her feet, 'I bet that's the wool from that jumper I've never finished. Never will now.'

'This *still* isn't ready,' Wolfe complains. 'I've been standing on this chair stirring for ages and ages.' Petra drops some toffee into the water. It hangs in wobbly strings. 'It's been doing that for ages,' Wolfe says.

'Oh well, perhaps it'll do,' Petra says. 'I've never got the hang of toffee. You really need a thermometer. I'll tip it into the tin.' She tips the pan and the black liquid hisses and the tin creaks and cracks with the sudden heat. 'We'll leave it now till it begins to set and then mark it into squares. When I was little we used to have a toffee hammer,' she says, her eyes far away. 'A little silver hammer specially made for breaking toffee into lumps.'

'A toffee hammer,' repeats Wolfe dreamily. 'It must have been good in those days.'

* * *

Olive kneels in the front bay windows, resting her elbows on the sill, watching the people passing by. Arthur is out the back tidying the garden and she can hear the sharp sporadic snap of his secateurs as he cuts back some shrub or other. She is waiting for him to come in because she is bored today and there is nothing for her. She tried with the book, she really did, but the doings of Mellstock choir among the creaking trees defeated her. There is nothing to do but wander from room to room, wander outside, struggle down, struggle up. She fingers a fleshy leaf belonging to one of Arthur's plants, the sort of thing that flowers at Christmas, she presses her nail against it and it goes through the thick skin leaving a moon-shaped slit, and green on the edge of her nail. She sighs. Stares out a passing woman who has the nerve to peer in. And then she sees something, something that makes her start, and then cry out.

'Artie! Artie!' Her voice comes out in a weak bleat, so that Arthur doesn't hear at first, so that by the time he has heard her and hurried in, her hat has gone again. For she has seen her hat. It was her hat but it was no human being that wore it. It had a mad, scribbled face, an evil face. The face of a witch's doll. And it had long black hair like her hair used to be, and red lips. 'It was me!' she cries out as Artie comes through the door.

'Whatever's up?' he says, kneeling down beside her. 'Calm down, me duck.'

'I'm telling you Artie, it was me. It was my hat. I saw it with some nasty children. It was my cherry hat, Artie, on some doll. Some doll they'd made to look like me!' She is breathless and trembling.

'Sit down on floor,' Arthur says. 'Lie down. I'll get cushion. I'll get kettle on and mash us a cup . . .'

'Artie! Aren't you listening?'

'Aye, I'm listening duck. You've had a shock.'

'Go and get them! Quick Artie, go out and look!'

Woodenly, Arthur gets up and goes out onto the street and looks up and down. As he expected there is no one about, only a woman with a pram, a cat stalking. He doesn't know, he just doesn't know any more what to believe. Olive could have seen her hat, someone wearing her hat. Or it could have been a different hat. Or maybe not a hat at all. Maybe nothing at all. He takes a long shuddery breath and goes back indoors.

'Nowt,' he says. 'They've gone. Were it a lad or a lass wearing hat?'

'It was me Artie, don't you understand. *Me*.'

'Oh . . .' Arthur's heart is a stone in his chest.

'Don't look at me like that Artie, as if I'm off my rocker. I saw it I tell you. They'd made it up to look like me, the buggers. And if you won't go out and search, I will!' She pulls herself to her feet and stands massive before Arthur, red-faced and trembling. Arthur steps back.

'All right, all right.' He will not be afraid of Olive, just because she is so heavy and cantankerous, just because reason doesn't come into it when she's in one of her rages. But he steps back. 'I'll fetch your coat,' he says. 'And then we'll take Potkins and go out together and look. Eh?' He goes to fetch Olive's coat and her outdoor shoes. 'Someone at door,' he calls, hearing a timid knocking.

He opens the door to Wolfe. 'I've just come to make sure you're coming to our bonfire party tonight,' Wolfe says all in one breath, 'only Mum wants to know how many potatoes to do and we've already made some toffee.'

'Is that right?' Arthur chuckles at the dark sticky ring round Wolfe's mouth. 'I'll just ask Olive. Ollie,' he calls. 'Lad next door's asking if we're going to firework party tonight.'

'You'll do what you want to do,' she says.

'We'll come,' he promises Wolfe, quietly.

'Great! Seven o'clock, Mum says. We're having a bonfire and a guy and everything.' Wolfe goes off, and Arthur helps Olive into her coat.

*   *   *

In the baker's, Nell buys a slab of parkin. She is excited and her fingers quiver in her purse. An invitation! It is the first for years. She's not so bad really, her next door, a bit slap-happy perhaps but properly neighbourly. And those children were quite charming this morning. They may be scruffy little urchins but she's taught them manners and that's what counts. It's as well to be broadminded – and after all, a party! Rodney is at the barber's now, and then she'll send him to see about some decent shoes. It's a long time since she's socialised. Well, Jim was never bothered, they were happy as they were. They

were all the company they needed, and there was the shared
shame of Rodney, no need to go spreading that about. And
times change, you don't know who you can trust nowadays,
but still . . . content as she is, she is pleased at the idea of a little
party with the kiddies next door. If only Rodney will not
disgrace her. If only he will behave properly. Still, she'll be
there to keep an eye. Nothing untoward can happen under her
very eyes.

The parkin is a heavy moist square in its paper bag. She's not
had parkin for years. Her mouth waters at the thought.
Although she's not sure whether she can touch the baker's
parkin, loose parkin, you can never be sure who's had their
hands on it. Still, her mouth waters at the memory. Pity Mr
Kipling doesn't do a slab of parkin, hygienic, sealed in a box.

Since Rodney grew up Bonfire Night has always been a trial,
all that banging and popping starting weeks before, hooligans
and vandals in the street with their bangers trying to frighten
the wits out of decent folk. But it will be controlled tonight, the
bonfire and the fireworks. Jim used to see to all that when
Rodney was a lad. She remembers it as if it was yesterday. The
rockets in their milk-bottles, the Catherine wheels nailed to the
gate post, herself and little Rodney holding woolly hands
while Jim in his rubber boots conducted the show.

She thinks of the blaze the silly hat will make, and her lips
twitch into a smile. That will be an end of it. Nell feels
triumphant. If only Father was alive. If only Father could see
the wreck his little Gyspy has become. If only Jim could see her
staggering down the street in her shabby coat, her hair a
colourless fuzz. Oh yes, it's taken years to feel it, practically a
lifetime, but Nell feels better. And she even has her son back
with her now. She has a child, a living child, unlike some.

*   *   *

'Remember remember the 5th of November, gunpowder, treason and plot,' Olive recites.

'And something and something and something and something, will never be forgot,' murmurs Arthur. A realisation is growing in his mind. Guy Fawkes, of course! It was a guy Olive must have seen, some kids carrying a guy. And it *could* have been her hat on the guy, or some other hat, but at least that makes sense of what Olive saw. He opens his mouth to say, but then thinks better of it. If the hat is on a guy somewhere, then that's that. It will be burnt. And to tell Olive that would only be to set her off again, as surely as holding a match to a rocket. He grimaces at the thought. Potkins will not give over pulling, and what with Olive's weight holding him back and the dog straining forward, he feels he will snap in two.

'See, Artie,' says Olive. 'See how he pulls.'

'I know Ollie. It's a wonder you managed at all.' They have reached the corner and stand looking down the hill.

'That's where I fell, just down there.' Olive points to a spot a little way down.

'Poor Ollie,' Arthur says. 'And you did come down a smack. It's a wonder there's no bones broken.'

'No sign of my hat,' Olive sighs.

'Look at them there chrysanths,' Arthur says. He gazes through a window at a vase of the great fat globes, rust and white and yellow, each bloom an ordered mass of frail tongues, big as a grapefruit.

'Never mind chrysanths,' Olive grumbles, but Arthur does mind. He's given them up lately, but there was a time when his were the best blooms on the allotment, and Jim's not far behind. Friendly competition it was, no spite in it, but they each had their own secrets. It was a sort of game between them. And every autumn on each of the window-sills, in the very centre of each of the bays, there would be a great boastful display of them, huge glowing rusty suns, fat and heavy as fruits. Oh yes, they had their own secrets. Arthur squeezes Olive's arm. There was one year, only one, when his were undoubtedly the finest. Indisputably. Most years there wasn't much in it, but this particular year . . . His cheeks pinch into a smile. He had the secret that year – Olive's pee. It was the year she was expecting. He doesn't know where he heard it, whether he picked it up in Norfolk, or what, but he'd heard that the water of a pregnant woman was like a magic elixir to chrysanthemums, and so when Olive was expecting he'd taken the golden stuff nightly from the china po under the bed, and he'd fed it to the plants and didn't it do the trick! Strong stems and blooms like lions' heads, proud and tawny.

'We'll go to the party tonight, you and me,' he decides, tugging both Kropotkin and Olive in the direction of home. 'It'll do you good, take you out of yourself for a bit.'

'If you say so.'

'I do say so. And we don't want to go letting lad down.'

'But what about Potkins, Artie? What about Mao? What will they make of all the banging and the crashing? All the flames and the whatsits.'

'Fireworks. We'll shut them up safe. We'll let Potkins in kitchen for tonight.' Kropotkin turns around and looks at him and grins through his grizzled lips.

Eight

Wolfe stands outside ready and waiting. He wears his boots and has his duffel-coat hood up against the damp air. It is a cloudy night, but there has been no rain. The fire is also ready and waiting, the guy on top, tied to the central pole. He is slumped, his head down on his chest, and Wolfe cannot meet his eye. He wears an old hat now. A squashed holiday hat, and he looks scruffy and poor. His lips are black in the little light coming from the kitchen window.

All down the hill in the small, fenced-off gardens, there are small fires, small groups of people having small parties. The air is already smoky and there is the occasional bang, the odd pale trail of a rocket in the sky. Wolfe thinks of how it would be at the Longhouse: a giant fire, someone playing the fiddle, people dancing perhaps, and shouting and laughing and drinking elderberry wine, warmed on the stove and spiced so that just breathing in the smell could make you feel drunk. But here all the fires are separate and private and everyone has a different guy to burn.

Tom comes out and stands beside him. 'All right, mate?'

'Course.'

'Can't wait to get started, eh?'

'No.'

'We'll light the fire in a mo, get a good blaze going before the fireworks. Tell you what, old mate, you can do the honours.'

'What honours?'

'You can light the fire. Fancy that?'

'If you like,' says Wolfe.

'What's up, Wolfie?'

'Nothing.' He doesn't like Tom using Petra's name for him.

It feels as if Tom is trying to get him to like him, trying too hard to be a friend.

'Pull the other one,' Tom says. 'Come on, what's up?'

'You never . . . nothing.'

'Come on, it's like pulling bleeding teeth!' Tom hugs Wolfe against him so that his nose is squashed against the roughness of Tom's jacket. Wolfe pulls away. 'Christ, I'm not that bad am I?'

'It's just that you never took me out when you said you would.'

'Oh that. Is that all? I'm sorry mate, that was out of line. I should have said. Tell you what, I'll take you with me, next chance I get.'

'Promise?'

'Promise.'

'And . . .' Wolfe struggles, 'it's just that I don't know about you. I never know whether you're going to be there. What if you leave us? What about Mum?'

Tom is silent for a moment, and his face gazing at the unlit fire is as serious and nearly as sad as the guy's. Then he shakes his head and sighs. 'I know it's rough, mate. But look, let's get the fire lit now. Come on,' he tries to make his voice sound cheerful, 'we're having a party.' He gives Wolfe a box of matches.

'But Mum says I mustn't . . .'

'It's all right, I'm – what do they say? – supervising. Just strike one and light the paper at the bottom in a few places.'

Wolfe opens the box and nervously strikes a match against its rough side. Nothing happens at first, just a grating sound. He strikes quicker and harder and there is a little spark.

'Have another shot,' Tom says, and Wolfe lights the match and almost drops it. 'That's it, now quick, before it burns your fingers.'

Wolfe holds the flaming match gingerly between his finger

and thumb. There is no time. He flicks a look at the lolling guy, at the black and silent mouth, and then he flings the match onto the paper and turns away.

'Hey . . . all right, light another one then,' Tom says, but Wolfe hands him back the matches. He wants to run away and not see the guy burning, but Buffy and Bobby come outside and he is trapped into being brave. He turns to face the fire. Tom has started the blaze going in several places around the bottom and the flames swiftly bud and blossom and lick upwards over the dry paper and wood. The guy's face is lit for a bright moment as the flames slither up, and his eyes meet Wolfe's, and Wolfe wants to cry out his sorrow. He wants to leap into the flames and save the guy, but then he sees that the the big red lips are open in a smile. It is like joy. The brim of the hat flares like a halo and just for a moment the face is blazing with joy. Just for a moment, and then it flickers black and warps and smokes and dissolves into feathers of ash fleeing upwards in the blasting heat.

'That is what he was for!' cries Wolfe.

'What's that?' says Tom, but Wolfe cannot speak, he is transfixed by the bright upward flow of the fire, the crackle and whoosh of it. The face has gone but the hat blazes on and the woollen hair frizzles to nothing and smoke.

'Good grief!' exclaims Petra coming outside with Nell and Rodney, 'that's gone off like a bomb!'

'Spot of turps makes all the difference,' Tom says.

'I don't think there was any need for that,' Petra grumbles. 'It was perfectly dry. Anyway Tom, this is Nell and Rodney . . .'

Wolfe half listens to the grown-up talk of weather, the offers of tea or wine, and he watches the flames. His face is hot, his cheeks baking like potatoes. The fire is beautiful and the guy is nothing now but a darkened ghost in the brightness below the flaring circle of the hat.

He feels a cold creeping on his back as if someone is
watching him, and he turns to see Rodney's eyes upon him.
Not his eyes, but the lenses of his glasses that reflect the leaping
flames.

Nell cannot concentrate on the chat. Oh she must chat, of
course, she must chat and she must be seen to sip her tea, but
how can she in the poor light, when she cannot see clearly
whether the cup is properly clean? The rim feels greasy against
her lips and her throat clamps shut because, of course, she
could never swallow strange tea out of a strange greasy cup in
the darkness. She scrubs the back of her hand against her lips.
She peers at the cup in the unruly firelight, and finds that her
worst suspicions are confirmed. There is a crack in the cup and
Lord-knows-what in there, living and breeding and dying and
rotting. Everyone knows that germs flock into the cracks of
cups and plates. She can almost feel the crawl of them against
her hand. She must chat and she must hold the swarming cup
and she must pretend to drink but she really wants to watch
the fire, to enjoy the burning of the hat. The guy has almost
gone now, there is just something that looks like a pair of feet
paddling in the flames, and there, of course, is the remains of
the hat, making a good display. Despite the cup, despite the
annoying buzz of conversation to which she must pay heed,
Nell feels a smile coming on. The hat has been cremated. There
is a fizzing and a popping in the fire which is sure to be the
stupid cherries.
    'Yes, lovely,' she says to Petra, and guesses from Petra's face
that she's made the wrong response, but however can she be
expected to concentrate with so much going on? For, of
course, there is also Rodney. She must be vigilant. She must
watch his every move – and there he is now sidling up to the
little boy with the outlandish name. It is all right, of course, for
he is cured, but still, better safe than sorry.

'Rodney,' she calls, sharply. 'Come and stand with me,' and he comes almost too meekly, too obediently, like a chastened spaniel, and Nell is embarrassed and gives a strangled laugh.

'The kids have been so excited,' Petra says, 'even Bobby who is *so* sophisticated and above us all.'

'Our Rodney was just the same,' Nell says, 'always a one for getting himself into a state. Christmas Eve he never slept a wink. Only he was scared of the rockets, weren't you Rodney? He always hid his little face in my coat, didn't you?' She squeezes Rodney's arm and forces a grunt from him. If only he had a bit more about him . . . Still, at least he is respectable now, with his newly barbered head and his gleaming spectacles and shoes.

'What about the fireworks?' calls Buffy from across the fire.

'We're waiting for the others,' Tom says. He is a very thin man with a thin cigarette, like a wisp of straw, dangling from the corner of his mouth. Even in this light he looks unkempt, and after all the trouble she's been to with Rodney. Horrible to think that his lips, nicotine and all, have probably drunk from the very cup she holds in her hand now. She thinks longingly of her rubber gloves.

'Others?' she asks Petra, politely.

'Oh, just Arthur and Olive,' Petra says. 'Would you like a top-up?'

'No, thanks all the same.' Nell's stomach performs a little flip. *Just* Arthur and Olive! Oh Jim, she thinks, oh Jim, why aren't you here? Stupid of me, stupid of me not to think. If Jim was here there would be something to hold onto, some support, for although she has Rodney firmly by the upper arm, she might as well be holding onto a gooseberry bush for all the good it does her. She breathes in deeply of the smoky air. Somewhere down the hill a rocket flares and dies, and she calms herself. There is nothing, after all, to fear. Rather, she should try to think of this evening as a triumph. She was here first, after all, looking neat and appropriate in her herring-bone tweed coat and her little fur-lined boots. How will Olive compare? And the blessed hat is gone. It's only a shame that Olive wasn't here to see. What a fuss she would have made! Old tart shrieking and carrying on with her loud mouth and her foul tongue. What a shame they couldn't have seen one of her performances, Petra and Tom, seen her in her true colours. *Not* a very suitable influence for the kiddies.

'I'll just rinse my cup,' Nell says in Petra's ear, holding it away so that Petra cannot see that it is still full.

'No need,' says Petra, who, despite her advanced condition, is sipping wine.

'No trouble,' Nell says firmly.

'Well, help yourself to another cup – there's a potful – or a glass of wine, it's all there.' Petra does not seem to care about another woman in her kitchen. Nell tips her tea quickly down behind the plastic washing-up bowl in the sink. It is just as she suspected. Filthy. The stainless steel of the sink and draining board is coated in a greasy film and round the base of the taps is a ring of brownish sludge that she can practically see seething. Nell cannot bring herself to touch the taps, not with her bare hands, so she just inverts the cup amongst the jumble of crockery and cutlery on the draining board. One more cup will hardly make any difference to this germs' paradise. The floor is sticky to walk upon and Nell thanks Heaven for her rubber boots. The window-sill is crammed with dying plants, mugs, matches, pens, a bottle of cough medicine all sticky and dark, some lego bricks, a jar of something with a label so stained it is impossible to read, a hairbrush clogged with hair. Nell tut-tuts, but she does feel a flicker of glee. If only Jim was here to see. It does show, the trouble she takes to keep her house nice. It is not a thankless task when you see the pigsties other people live in. It's only surprising they're not always coming down with something. There must be plenty of things to come down with on the draining board alone.

And on the table near the food there is actually an ashtray containing a couple of skinny brown-stained cigarette ends! Really! If only Jim *was* here to say something nice about her own housekeeping. She looks closely at the food, all exposed to the open air. Anyone would think cling-film had never been invented. There's a plate of something brown and oozing, a salad, a bowl of grated cheese, some pickles still in their jars and a tub of margarine with crumbs in it. The oven is on and there's a not unpleasant smell of potatoes baked in their (no doubt grubby) jackets. Nell's own Tupperware box is there too, the parkin cut into neat squares, a most suitable contribution. There is a big bottle of red wine opened and a glass beside it, but she will not risk it. Besides, she must keep her wits about her. Rodney accepted a glass of wine rather too readily, and she must keep tabs on him.

They stagger into the garden like some kind of comedy double-act. Fatty and Skinny. Laurel and Hardy. Little and Large. Only they are for real, and far from funny. The thought of them together – it makes Nell squirm. Geriatric sex, surely not? Though she wouldn't put it past Olive. Fat tart; never a one to stick within decent limits. *And* they've come empty-handed. She thinks smugly of her parkin.

Unaccountably, the little boy runs to Arthur and takes his hand; Nell grasps Rodney again. Petra fetches Olive and Arthur glasses of wine, brimming black in the poor light. Nell has had enough of the chilliness and the smokiness and the griminess. Now that the hat is burnt there seems little point in the fire. A silliness in the little back garden, along with all the other sillinesses blazing down the hill. If only they'd get on with the fireworks, then they could decently get off home and wash their hands and have a proper cup of tea.

'Grand fire,' Arthur says, and Olive, buttoned into a bulging coat, says nothing at all, but stares rudely at Nell until she is made to feel uncomfortable and to fiddle and twitch with her hair.

Arthur squints into the flames. 'Did you burn your guy?' he asks.

'Yep. He's all gone now,' Wolfe says.

'Hat and all,' chips in Nell in a spiteful, needling voice. Arthur wishes Nell no good at all. He looks at Olive, but she does not appear to have heard. And it may not have been *the* hat, after all. And if it was? Mentioning it would only make trouble, only stir Olive up. And if by chance it was these children that found the cherry hat on the street and burnt it on their guy – well then it's good and gone and there's an end of it. At least Olive didn't see, at least she was spared that.

Wolfe's hand is sticky and rough in his own, like a little paw. 'We can start the fireworks now!' he says, looking up at Arthur from inside his hood.

'Now that we're all here,' says Nell.

'I thought . . .' begins Wolfe and then flounders for words.

'Go on, lad.'

'I thought it would be a shame to set the fireworks off and spoil them and not have them any more.'

'But that's what they're for!' Arthur chuckles.

'Yeah! And the guy, that was what he was for wasn't it? For burning.'

'That's it, me duck.' Arthur smiles down at him. A funny lad, a thinker – deep.

'I'm going to help,' Wolfe says, disengaging his hand. 'I want to choose what first.' He goes off to join in the argument already brewing between the others.

Olive is a heavy presence at Arthur's side. Her eyes are sparks in the firelight. There is a brightness in them that reminds him, almost, of how they used to flash; how they used to tease; how they used to lead him on and how good it was when he got there. He feels a stir of nostalgic excitement, unexpected, out of place here at a bonfire party; but still, a little hardening, remembering Ollie and the way she used to move. *And the darkness of the cleft between her buttocks as she knelt before him.* She was no ordinary lover, Olive, no wifey lover, not cold like that poor bitch Nell. *Oh and the soft looseness of Olive's big breasts cupped in his hands, the gentle prodding of her nipples.* He can just imagine what Nell would have been like in bed. Cold. A cold pair of scissors – stainless steel – open for a moment, out of duty, and then snap shut and God help you if you're not finished. It's a wonder they ever conceived Rodney. Poor bugger Jim. No wonder he turned to Olive. Arthur watches her sipping her wine. Her chin trembles. She is all looseness now, all softness – though inside she has grown hard with her resistance to what must be. And the fire lights her eyes like a breeze fanning slumbering coal. There is a tension growing in the air between Olive on his one side and Nell on the other. He almosts vibrates between them.

And now the children are ready with the fireworks.

'Golden Rain,' announces Wolfe. 'Light the blue touch-paper, Tom, and stand well back.'

Tom strikes a match and sets the thing aflame and then there is a wait, and then a sigh as if it has gone out, and then a gradual drizzle and spray of gold rising like a fountain and splashing onto the grass.

'Aaaah,' they say together. And Olive clutches Arthur's arm.

'Of course, my Jim was the one to talk to about fireworks,' Nell's voice rises as the firework dies. Tom bends to light the Traffic Lights.

'*Her* Jim,' mutters Olive.

'Hush,' says Arthur.

'Green!' cries Wolfe as the first soft pompon of light rises in the air.

'Always the best for Rodney, the best that money could buy,' continues Nell, but nobody pays her any attention. She has hold of Rodney, weird Rodney, middle-aged now. And how did the sweet bright boy who used to sear Arthur's heart with his very aliveness turn into this queer figure? Nell's stamp is on him again. He has a scoured look. His hair is fiercely short, his neck pale and naked where the razor has scraped. Nell had always been a one for cleanliness, even before the trouble with Rodney. But that had sent her funny, Jim had said. He'd told Arthur how it played on his mind. Always cleaning she was, always scrubbing, as if she was trying to scrub the shame away. Poor Nell. But whatever must it be to have a son who did such evil? Whatever must it be to have a son at all? Which, he wonders, is worse: the absence or the terrible presence? Again the memory of the tender fluffy head and the tiny fingers curled around his thumb.

'Orange!' Wolfe cries.

'Amber, dick – Stupid,' says his brother.

'Red next!'

And then again, to have a lad like Wolfe, a funny lad, fat and serious, innocent and wise. A special lad. He sighs.

'Oh the times we had! The parties! The fun when Rodney was a child!' crows Nell, and Arthur feels for Rodney who flinches against the lies, against the pincers of his mother's fingers on his arm. But there is no expression on his face, just a straight black line for a mouth and the flames of his glasses.

'Wolfe, why don't you hand around your toffee?' calls Petra who looks dangerously pregnant to Arthur, her belly jutting from between the edges of her coat.

'All right, but wait for me. Don't light any more till I'm ready.'

'Another drink anyone?' Petra offers.

'Me,' says Olive quickly. 'I'll have another.' Nell's eyes rise to Heaven.

'Go easy, duck,' Arthur murmurs to Olive, but he takes her glass and goes to Petra for a refill.

'We'll eat after the fireworks,' Petra says. 'Only don't get excited, it's only spuds.

Arthur hands Olive her drink. 'All right?' he says. She has her dangerous look. Wolfe thrusts forth the plate of toffee.

'Olive'll have a bit,' Arthur says. The toffee has melted upon the plate, trying to revert from separate lumps into one mass, and Arthur prizes a piece free with difficulty. 'Looks like a good old jaw-sticker,' he says.

Olive hangs on to Arthur. The sense has gone again, the meaning of all this. All these people, oh yes, some of them are known, some of them, and children too all lit with flames, all blinking with the smoke in their eyes. Arthur is here, at least, and there is a form on the fire like a human form, only faint, only a waver of smoke against the flame, perhaps it is nothing at all. And in her hand is a drink and her teeth are stuck together with toffee. And beside Arthur is Nell and her long face is a face of stone, a face of stone carved on a church porch somewhere and beaten away with the rain. It is an old face but the spite in it is young and green. The spite is there in the flickering of the flames lighting her face from beneath so that her nostrils are cavernous and the lines dragging down from her nose to the corners of her mouth are etched deep and black and her mouth opens and shuts like a trap and she talks of Jim. *Her* Jim.

Oh oh oh Olive knows Jim, knew Jim, *knew* Jim. And he loved Olive, oh yes he did, he loved her in every way, every way. He was such a big man, big body, bigger and hotter and clumsier than Arthur. He stuffed her so full she used to cry out with a sort of startled joy and she cries out now through the toffee so that they look at her, all of them, and Nell doesn't know what that sound means, and Arthur begins to fret. Big fingers he had too, gentle. But he never understood the rules, if they were rules – for was it a game or was it serious? Oh don't ask that, that is one too many for now. He could never understand that Arthur was Olive's and Olive was Arthur's and the physical thing was all that she wanted, the sensation of him, and it wasn't supposed to be a secret, that Arthur *knew* and that Arthur had other lovers too. He couldn't understand all that so it had to be kept secret from Nell, and that made it furtive. And although she loved – more than that, respected – Arthur, although he was her comrade, they stood back to back against the world, although she *loved* Arthur, part of her melted towards Jim, who talked of their running away together until Olive had to set herself against him, and force herself to laugh and tell him to run back to Nell if he wanted to run anywhere. And he did. And so she turned back to Arthur and all that he meant to her. And although she was quite certain that Jim was the father of her child, Arthur thought *he* was. He *was* in all the ways that matter. No one knew any better. It was kinder that way. She had thought it was kinder, all for the best. But all these years Arthur has mourned a son who was not his own and there is pain inside her that tells her she was wrong. But she cannot tell him now. She cannot take away that six-week trace of fatherhood. She cannot bereave him afresh.

The Catherine wheel will not spin properly. Tom prods it with a broom-handle and the children scream, 'Don't, don't!' and despite Tom's efforts it will only flip over in a bright little arc and then stick again, squirting its sparks onto the ground.

'They always do that,' grumbles Petra. 'I've never known a Catherine wheel to spin right yet. Never mind, Tom, let's have the rockets.'

'Of course,' begins Nell, 'my Jim had the secret of Catherine wheels. A loose nail through the centre . . .'

'*My* Jim,' scoffs Olive, loudly.

'Hush Ollie,' pleads Arthur, but his heart sinks. He knows the signs, the look in her eyes, the heaviness of her stance. She has gathered her wits and her temper is up.

'*My* Jim . . . oh if only you knew. There's things I know about *your* Jim would wipe that look off your face.'

Nell looks away sharply. 'Well then, perhaps the rockets,' she says to Petra in a stifled voice.

'Yes. Tom,' says Petra hastily.

'Mine first,' begs Wolfe.

'I had him,' Olive boasts. 'Oh yes, I had him and he was a bugger for it, wasn't he Nell? Did he give it to you like he gave it to me? A big bugger, wasn't he?'

There is a silence broken only by Bobby sniggering.

'I'm sorry,' says Arthur. 'She's not herself . . . perhaps we ought to . . .'

'Not myself!' cries Olive, 'not myself! What sort of rubbish is that? I'm more my –' but the toffee has done for her teeth and they fly out with the force of her passion to click to the ground.

'Wheee!' exclaims Petra desperately as Wolfe's rocket whizzes into the sky and feathers down its sparks of green and silver and blue. Arthur lets go of Olive's arm and bends to retrieve the glistening dentures.

'Talk about stretch,' continues Olive, unbashed, in a flabby voice. Now that she is free of Arthur she moves threateningly towards Nell.

'Really!' she says, superior in her fright. Arthur tries to grab Olive's arm but she shakes him off.

'Buffy's rocket,' announces Tom, but everyone is watching the lumbering form of Olive, massive in her bulging coat, advancing towards Nell who clings to a wilting Rodney.

'She's not herself,' pleads Arthur in her defence. 'Come on, Ollie, home now, come on, duck.'

Olive stumbles and drops her glass. It shatters and the wine bleeds away into the black ground. She hesitates and looks round for Arthur. It has gone now, the temper, and she is confused. 'Artie?' she says. Relieved, he goes to her and takes her arm.

'There now,' he says. 'Home now, I think . . . Sorry about glass,' he adds to Petra.

'Don't worry. Sure you don't want to stay for a potato?'

'I think we'd best get back.'

'Bye-bye,' calls Wolfe, sadly. Arthur leads Olive out of the gate and down the passage and as they leave he hears the voices drifting after them.

'Brilliant!' says Bobby, 'I thought she was going to land . . .'

'Shhh.'

'Poor old dear,' Nell's voice is tremulous but loud and carrying. 'All too much for her I suppose. What nonsense she does speak . . . delusions you know . . .'

'I'm sure,' says Petra, comforting, relieved. 'Now, what about Buffy's rocket?'

The fireworks are finished, the fire relaxing into its embers, the potatoes eaten. Wolfe wanders into the kitchen. He licks his finger and presses it into the corners of the Tupperware box to collect the crumbs. He sucks his fingers. They taste of ginger and smoke.

'Still hungry?' asks Rodney, who is suddenly there behind him.

'Me? No,' Wolfe replies. He turns round, his back to the table.

'Boys are always hungry,' Rodney says as if he hasn't heard. 'Boys like to eat.'

Rodney's ears stick out and they are very pink with the light shining through them, like fatty bits of bacon. There are bristles in his ears and his nose, and on the end of his nose is a drip. 'Didn't you like the fireworks? Were you scared of the bangs?' Rodney is drinking wine from the glass and his lips have left smeary marks on it. He fingers are funny at the ends, thin and flat like spades.

'I'm not scared at all,' Wolfe says. 'Course I'm not.'

'A brave boy then,' Rodney smiles. 'How old are you?'

'Me? I'm eight.'

'Only a little boy, for eight,' Rodney says.

'Well I am eight,' Wolfe says, and then because he likes to be polite, 'only I do look younger, everyone says.'

'And you've got poor sore hands . . .' Rodney puts down his glass and reaches out his hands to Wolfe but Wolfe puts his behind his back. Rodney lets his hands drop sadly to his sides, and Wolfe is sorry. 'Have you been to see the Cutlers' Wheel?' Rodney asks.

Wolfe shakes his head. Rodney's head looks too small for his tall body, tiny, almost pointed, with its huge ears, and he leans it now towards Wolfe and his lips are very wet and his eyes flicker behind his glasses.

'No. What is it?'

'Through the park, through the woods, over the bridge to the Cutlers' Wheel. Where they used to grind cultery. Water power. It's a grand sight. Grand sound. Water rushing and the great wheel – all rust and moss now but still working – and the belts all rattling away inside.'

'Oh . . . no, I've never heard of it.'

'You must see it. Would you like to see it? Rodney could take you to see it.'

Wolfe hesitates. The drip on the end of Rodney's nose drops.

'It's all right, thanks, I'll ask my mum to take me.'

'No . . . if you go first, then you can surprise your mum, tell

her all about it, show her the way, take her to see it.' He is
nervous, Wolfe sees, his eyes jumping, his fingers fiddling with
his glass. Perhaps he is lonely, like Wolfe. Perhaps he wants to
make friends. Wolfe knows how horrible it is to have no
friends, and Rodney looks the type of person people might
make fun of. Big Ears, they might call him, or Blubber Lugs, or
Four Eyes.

'All right then,' says Wolfe. After all, although he is strange,
Rodney is not a stranger but a neighbour. It is strangers that
you must say no to.

'When?' asks Rodney. His mother comes into the kitchen.
Wolfe sees the way she stares at Rodney, her face sharp as a
beak.

'When what?' she demands.

'Nothing,' says Rodney.

Nell looks at Wolfe. 'Nothing,' he agrees.

'Yes,' Nell looks from Rodney to Wolfe and then takes
Rodney's arm. 'Well anyway, you can come outside with me
where I can keep an eye on you.'

Wolfe, left alone in the kitchen, grimaces, and goes back to
licking the last crumbs from Nell's box. He'd die if his mother
spoke to him like that in front of someone else. Especially if he
was grown up.

* * *

'Mao,' Olive calls from her bed. 'Artie, where's Mao?' Arthur
swallows. He'd hoped that Olive hadn't noticed the absence of
the cat.

'He's all right,' he evades, stepping out of his trousers.

'But where?'

'He went out.'

'Out? Artie, out? On a night like this!' Olive struggles to a
half-sitting position.

'He'll be all right. Don't fuss.'

'But the bombs Arthur! The bombs and the blazes . . .'

'Fireworks is all they are. He'll be all right. He'll be holed up somewhere and back in morning, you see.'

'But Arthur he'll freeze! You must go out and search . . .'

'No, Olive,' says Arthur sharply, and he never speaks sharply to her and she stops, about to speak, with her mouth open. 'And you were bad this evening,' Arthur continues. 'Didn't know where to put myself when you went off like that. Language like that! And with the kids there too.'

'Bloody old buggering bitch,' says Olive reflectively.

'No excuse . . . I don't know what got into you.'

'The way she talks about him as if he was some sort of apostle. He liked a good . . .'

'Ollie!' Arthur climbs into bed beside her and unwillingly rolls down into her warmth. She snuggles and murmurs. 'What am I going to do with you?' he sighs. She is dreadful, a dreadful woman with a filthy tongue and he is angry with her, and he is excited by her. She will never give up. She gets worse. He rolls on top of her. She smells of bonfires and sweet toffee and there is a faint taste of wine on her lips. She is endlessly big and soft and he burrows himself down into her, kissing and squeezing and kneading her. She moans luxuriously.

'Oh yes, Artie, that is what you do with me, that's it,' and together they rock in a familiar pleasure, a tender crumpled pleasure that ends not in fierce spurts of passion, not in ecstatic cries, but in a gentle dribble of content, a mutual slowing to a stop.

'There, there, my bad lass, my wicked lass,' murmurs Arthur, but Olive is already slipping through into the deep of her sleep. 'Sweet dreams.'

Olive, softly, snores.

* * *

'A *good* wash, mind,' says Nell. 'Fires spread dirt right through the air, and it was none too clean inside, though *you* wouldn't have noticed I *don't* suppose. *And* the state of that cup! How she expected me to drink out of *that*! *And* her in the family way.' Rodney looks vacantly at Nell.

'And Olive made a proper fool of herself tonight, didn't she, Rodney? Didn't she? Pitiful really. Talking such stuff and nonsense about your father. Mad. Senile, that's what she is, spouting those filthy lies. Fantasies I'd call them. Such filthy fantasies about your father! Oh she really went too far. Whatever must they think? It almost makes me feel sorry for her. And in front of the children too!'

Nell is light-hearted, excited, almost happy. She smiles at Rodney. 'Get a move on then. Shoes off and have a wash and then I'll get the kettle on for a decent cuppa.' She washes her hands under the kitchen tap. 'Praise where praise due though, Rodney, I must say I was proud . . . well not ashamed of you tonight, Rodney, with your hair cut and all. He made a tidy job of it, that barber.'

Rodney bends to untie his shoes.

'Put them on a bit of newspaper by the door, that's it. And what was it you were saying to that little lad in the kitchen?'

'Nothing much,' Rodney moves towards the teapot.

'No, leave that. I'd as soon do it myself. I'll have a biscuit, I think. You? A proper wash now, the soap's there.' She watches the water flowing over Rodney's hands. 'I didn't fancy those potatoes – I've never seen the point of leaving the dirty old skins on – but now we're back I'm not sure I'm not a bit peckish. I'm not saying you're not to be trusted, Rodney, I'm not saying that, but you just stay away from the lad next door, from all of them. Understand?'

'Yes.'

'What did you think of them, next door?'

'Not bothered.'

'Well, that's all right then.' Nell reaches down the biscuit tin. 'There's no call to be getting what your father would have called over-friendly, always best to keep a distance.'

'Lead us not into temptation,' Rodney mutters.

'What's that?'

'Part of a prayer. The Lord's Prayer. Deliver us from evil.'

'Oh yes, well, no harm in a prayer I dare say, but just you . . .'

'He knows.' Rodney's face is flushing. His hands are dripping on the floor and he never used the soap after all that, but Nell holds her tongue. She pours the boiling water into the pot and scratches a little spot off the sink with her thumbnail as she waits for it to brew.

'Where they think they're going to put another child, I don't know,' she says. 'It'll be like sardines in there by the time they've finished. I don't know what your father would have said . . .'

'Leave them be, Nell.'

'What?' asks Nell, startled.

'That's what Dad would have said – if he'd said anything at all.'

Nell stalks round the bedroom in her long nightdress. Her hair is still damp from her bath and trapped to her head in a tight mesh cap. Her long bony feet are cold from pacing the floor, but she cannot be still. She is recounting to Jim every detail, every word, every speck of dust, and his eyes follow her around the dim bedroom from his sunny frame.

'And that Arthur, such a dried-up old fogey he is. How he still copes with his allotment I *don't* know. He's not up to it, Jim, never has been if you ask my opinion, not like you were.'

'Why not get into bed, my love?' suggests Jim mildly. 'Hop in now. You must be frozen.'

'And her next door in the family way. Did I say, Jim? And

did I see a wedding ring? Did I heck. And that Olive . . . oh that precious Olive . . . well I don't know where to start. It's all lies. Of course, I don't need to ask because it's all lies, isn't it, Jim? I know you thought she was a looker with her lips all red like I don't know what – but she was obvious, wasn't she? You always said she was obvious. And it's all lies. Of course, it's all lies. And the precious hat, well that's all ashes now. Those children burnt it. I wasn't to know they'd burn it, was I. And it was all lies, wasn't it? Wasn't it?' Nell's voice has risen to an anxious bray but Jim is silent. He does that, could always do that, go silent all of a sudden, shut off. It enrages Nell that he can do that, withdraw like a snail into its shell just when her anger is rising. Of course, he is right. It is never a good thing to display anger, or any passion for that matter. Especially not in public, but not in private either, for one must always be in control. Not like Olive. All that loud laughter, shouting, crying even, in public, and look at her now, not even in control of her teeth let alone her emotions.

'Well anyway, she's properly senile now, the old tart,' she hisses. 'How could you ever have looked at her . . . and that nincompoop Arthur stuck with her. Stuck with a fat old geriatric trollop. Twenty stone she must be, no exaggeration Jim, and me still only nine. And you should have seen the performance she put on tonight! The filth that came out of that mouth! And it's not true, is it Jim, no I needn't ask. Of course it isn't true. Is it? Is it? Why can't you just . . .' And the anger wells like a balloon expanding in her chest. But she will be calm, she must be, must be calm. She breathes in deeply, counts the seconds, breathes deeply of the cold, reassuringly Dettol-scented air.

'Hop into bed, love,' Jim advises again from the heaven of his frame.

Nell sits down before her dressing table and gazes at her bony face in the mirror. She will be calm. In the mirror her face is calm. She thinks calming thoughts. 'Now if Olive had had children, had children that lived . . .' That thought calms her. 'Oh you really should see her, Jim, you should see her now. You wouldn't look twice now, you'd look away. And I'm not so bad for my age, not so bad, not an ounce more than on our wedding day.'

Nell's mind drifts back to her wedding day. Her face softens at the memory. She had married young, the first man to propose, a man some few years older, not a boy, a proper man. A man her father approved of: Jim. She had been a tall willow of a girl and her dress had been of creamy crêpe de Chine. Like a fragile blossom she'd been, and she'd held her father's arm as they'd walked outside the church, and he had squeezed her hand and smiled complicitly, smiled his approval, and she'd trembled then in perfect happiness, perfect fulfilment. That was probably the best moment of her life, she realises, surprised, that tiny moment alone with her father, waiting for the organ to strike up. Poised between the two men in her life, on the boundary between daughter and wife, trembling on the brink.

The day had been perfect, long shafts of sunshine penetrating the dim church interior, seeming to bless their union. And afterwards wine and cold meats and cake, and then the speeches and the toasts; and Edwin seeming suddenly young and gauche and Nell smiling generously upon him from her exalted position. Olive had been there too, dressed in something tawdry and rayon, with a smudge upon her cheek no doubt, but for once all eyes had been on Nell.

It was only afterwards, towards the evening when the air was growing chill, that she had overheard her father say to someone, 'Well that's her off my hands for good and all,' as if she was not so much a fragile blossom as a troublesome puppy. She had turned away then, pretending not to have heard. And it was her own fault: after all, eavesdroppers never hear good

of themselves, and he probably hadn't meant it. It was just the
sort of thing fathers-of-the-bride say at weddings, and so she
had smiled bravely and gone to look for Jim, husband Jim. In
her memory sometimes now, the faces of her father and of Jim
become curiously confused, the one superimposed upon the
other. It strikes her how alike they were.

She turns to Jim, and brushes her fingers against her lips and
then against his frame. 'Good-night, my dear,' she says.

Nine

'Mum, there's a frozen chicken in the garden!' shrieks Wolfe. Tom is in bed with Petra, and both raise their heads slightly and peer at him over the quilt.

'Don't be daft,' Petra mutters and flops back. Tom moans, turns over and buries his face in the pillow.

'There is, honest, you look if you don't believe me.'

'Eight o'clock, Mum,' calls Buffy. 'Aren't you getting up? It's school. Bobby's gone.'

'Oh Christ,' Tom murmurs.

'What's the matter?' Wolfe sits on the side of the bed, looking at the little he can see of Petra. Her eyes are closed again and her hair is streaked stickily across her forehead.

'We were up half the night,' she whispers through dry lips. 'False alarm.'

'Alarm?'

'False . . . nothing doing?'

'What do you mean?'

'Oh nothing, never mind. Are you ready for school? Ask Buffy to bring us a cup of tea, will you?'

'I'm not going to school. My skin's bad, look.' Wolfe holds his poor scaly hands in front of her face. The skin is thick and red and cracked and weeping. 'I'm sorry. I've been trying not to scratch.'

'Oh no,' Petra squints at his hands. 'Oh no . . . that's all we need. Poor Wolfie, I wonder what brought that on?'

'And what about the chicken?'

'What chicken?'

'The one on the lawn, I told you.'

Buffy comes in. 'It's gone eight,' she complains. 'Aren't you getting up?'

'Bring us a cup of tea, love,' pleads Petra.

'Have you seen the frozen chicken on the lawn?' asks Wolfe.

'Don't be daft,' says Buffy, admiring herself in the mirror, 'we're vegetarian.'

'We're not. We eat fish and chips.'

'But not chicken.'

'Anyway look out of the window.' Buffy pulls a face at him before she draws back the curtain and looks out. 'I can't see . . . oh wait a minute, there is something . . . and it does look a bit like a chicken. Plucked.'

'See, told you so!'

'Tea,' Petra begs weakly.

'Coming up, the kettle's boiled.' Buffy clatters downstairs. Tom sits up, yawns and stretches to reveal wads of thick damp black hair in his armpits. Wolfe looks away.

'And the backs of my knees are bad, too,' he says. 'I must have been scratching in my sleep . . . look . . .'

'OK, OK, you'd better stay off today,' Petra says, opening her eyes properly at last.

'Come into town with me, mate,' Tom says. 'I'm going to do a picture.'

'And you can pick Wolfie up some more cream from the chemist's while you're at it.'

'But what if someone sees me in town when I'm meant to be ill?' asks Wolfe. It is bad enough with none of the kids at school liking him without getting into trouble with the teachers too.

'Don't worry,' says Petra, 'I'll write you a note. Anyway . . .'

'Anyway what?' But Tom has silenced her with a look. 'What? insists Wolfe. Tom raises an eyebrow at him.

'Pass me my glasses, mate,' he says.

'State of flux again?' Wolfe asks grumpily.

'That's about the size of it. Clever little bleeder aren't you?'
Tom smiles at him in a warm way, quite a friendly way, and
Wolfe half forgives him for letting him down.

'Can I come into town with you then?'

'Sure you can.'

'Here you are.' Buffy pushes through the door with two
slopping mugs of tea. 'And get this . . .' she dashes downstairs
again and returns with a bald cat. 'Here's your chicken,
Wolfe.' She drops it on the bed. 'I'm off.' She bends over and
kisses Petra. 'Look after Nothing, Mum.'

Wolfe looks at the creature with a mixture of wonder and
pity. It is a bluish colour, smudged with grey ash, and its skin is
smooth as a baby's. Its sharp ribs, knobby spine and the points
of its leg bones show yellow through the stretched skin. Its face
is weird like a space creature's, half human, half cat, grey-
white and stretched and wrinkled at the same time. It blinks
blue eyes at Wolfe, clever eyes, not frightened at all, and then it
creeps towards him, its skin cold against his own.

'It's frozen, poor thing,' Petra observes, sipping her tea.

'It's bloody disgusting,' Tom says. 'What is it do you think, a
freak, or bred like that?'

'No idea.'

'Well it gives me the willies,' Tom says, and Wolfe giggles.
The cat begins to purr, a high-pitched clockwork sound.

'And before you start,' Petra says, 'we're not keeping it.
We're already landed with Buffy's kitten.'

*   *   *

'First my hat and then my cat,' moans Olive. 'What's
happening, Artie?'

'Nowt, Ollie. We'll find him.' Arthur stands at the back
door looking out, hoping that the half-witted creature hasn't
gone and frozen to death somewhere. He wears his corduroys

and holds the godstone in his hand. 'I'll go out and look in a bit.' Today, somehow, he must get up to the allotment, just for an hour, just to see whether the bean seedlings are showing yet. He must get up there to breathe, and to think. 'I'll fetch a few parsnip back today,' he says, 'and I'll make a stew for your tea. Fetch some scrag-end from butcher. Eh Ollie?'

'All right, Artie, as long as you find Mao. Poor little blighter. He'll be crying. He'll be wanting his breakfast.' She tucks greedily into her own bread and lime marmalade. 'He'll have been frightened by the, by the, by the . . .'

'Fireworks,' supplies Arthur. 'Maybe, maybe not. He'll be back. Don't fret, Ollie, he'll be back, you wait and see. And it weren't cold last night. No frost.'

'And I was terrible last night, wasn't I, Artie? You said I was terrible. A disgrace.'

'You were that, Ollie,' agrees Arthur sternly. She catches his eye and together they laugh.

*   *   *

Tom kneels on the pavement of the city-centre shopping precinct. He has roughed out the shape of a leaping fish, a salmon, on the smooth paving stones and now he shades intently, the chalk-dust billowing around him and speckling his wire-rimmed glasses and his black curly hair. Already people are gathering to watch, and Wolfe feels proud to be a part of it. Before he started, Tom put a few coins in an old hat – to get the ball rolling, he said, and he gave Wolfe some coins too and told him to wander about, stroll past, and toss a few in now and again to encourage the other punters, that's what he called them, punters. But Wolfe is fascinated, rooted to the spot watching Tom's chalky fingers busying away, watching the white and blue and green and yellow and pink of the separate chalks mixing and blurring and then becoming a fat

glistening salmon, leaping upwards against the water streaming down.

'It's a fish!' cries a little girl.

'Isn't it lovely,' her mother says, resting her shopping bags
on the ground, and Wolfe swells with pride.

'I could fancy a bit of fish for my dinner,' says another, and
Tom looks up and winks at Wolfe.

'That's grand, lad, first-class,' a man says, and Wolfe walks
away and back and flings his money into the hat and it is
followed by a few other embarrassed clinkings.

'That'll do.' Tom stands stiffly up. 'Oh my knees,' he groans,
'it does them in kneeling like that . . . and my back.' He puts his
hand to the small of his back, leaving a chalky smudge.

'What do you think?' he asks Wolfe. They both stand
looking at it critically for a moment.

'Brilliant,' Wolfe says. 'I wish I could draw like that.
Nothing ever looks right when I draw.'

'Not so bad, is it? You'll learn. I had to learn, I wasn't much
cop at drawing myself when I was your age.'

'Really?'

'The secret is, you have to get inside when you're drawing,
get inside whatever it is. Bloody exhausting it is. I feel like I've
been hurling myself upwards all morning, pushing up against
the weight of that water.'

Wolfe gazes at the glistening fish and then at Tom. 'I've
never thought of it like that,' he says.

'Well, there you are then.' Someone flings a handful of silver
into the hat. 'Thanks, mate,' Tom calls. 'Go in the Wimpy and
get me a coffee,' he says to Wolfe, scooping some coins out of
the hat, 'and get yourself a Coke or whatever.'

Wolfe goes off feeling bigger then usual, swollen with
importance, off school, spending the morning with an artist,
and an artist who is practically his father. He has to reach up to
pay for the drinks, and he notices the way the woman who

serves him looks at his scabby cream-smeared hands, but he doesn't care. He feels happier than he has for ages. When he gets back, Tom is talking to a very small woman.

'Hello,' Wolfe says. She has curly brown hair and big eyes and a little nose, turned up at the end, like a pretty pig's.

'This is Petra's child?' she asks Tom, in a voice that is not English.

Tom nods. 'Wolfe. This is Eva,' he explains to Wolfe. 'A friend.' She seems to be a very good friend. She laughs a lot and she touches Tom's arm and never takes her eyes off him.

'How about a drink?' she asks him.

'Not today . . . I've got the kid.' Wolfe scowls at them, shrunk back into just a child, a nuisance.

'He could wait outside,' Eva says, wrinkling her little nose at Tom. 'You wouldn't mind that, would you, Woof?'

'Wolfe,' Wolfe says crossly, 'and I *would* mind.'

'Good on you,' Tom says, grinning at him. 'Anyway, Eva, I'm sticking around a bit longer. More room in the hat yet.'

'It will only rain,' Eva says, 'and ruin your wonderful fish.' She pouts her lips.

Tom shrugs. 'That's the way it goes.'

'If that's how you feel,' Eva says. She stands on tiptoe in her brown boots and kisses Tom crossly on the lips. 'You know where I am.' They both watch her walk away. Her jeans are very tight. She is about the half the size of Petra.

'Who's she?' Wolfe demands.

'Just someone.'

'Where does she come from?'

'Oslo . . . Norway.'

'Why did she kiss you?'

'Don't ask me.' Tom takes a sip of coffee out of the polystyrene cup and pulls a face. 'Crap,' he grumbles. 'And that's enough of the third degree. And you needn't mention Eva to your mum.'

'Why not?'

'Because she wouldn't understand.'

'Understand what?'

'Oh mate, just take my word for it, all right? I'm knackered.
Been up all bleeding night.'

'What is a false alarm, anyway?'

'We thought the baby was coming early . . . got in a proper
tizz. She decided she didn't want to go into hospital, and we
had a bit of a barney . . . and then anyway it stopped, thank
Christ. We were up the rest of the night talking. We got off to
sleep just before you lot woke us up this morning.'

'Is that what Mum was going to say this morning?
Something about what you'd been talking about?'

'Yes, that's it.' Tom drains his cup, grimaces again and then
screws it up in his hand.

'What was it?'

'Well . . . ' Tom hesitates. 'I suppose you'll know sooner or
later. It's not working out . . . '

Wolfe feels suddenly cold and sick. He looks at the salmon
struggling like a landed fish on the pavement. 'So you are
leaving us.'

'No, it's all right, me old mate, don't look like that!' Tom puts
his arm around him. 'What I mean is, it's not working out *here*,
like this. Your mum's been a bit down. She hasn't got any mates
here, and she hasn't been feeling like getting out much . . . '

'I haven't got any mates either.'

'No. That's another thing she's been worrying about. What
with her fretting about you being unhappy at school and your
skin flaring up again; and us worrying about this baby, well
. . . ' Wolfe holds his breath. 'We're thinking of moving. All of
us together. I've been here long enough, anyway. Quite fancy
moving on. We're staying together, Pet and me – and you kids
– but not here.' More money clinks into the hat. 'Thanks,' calls
Tom, and lifts his hand in a friendly wave.

'Thanks,' says Wolfe.

'I haven't told you this,' Tom says, 'understand? But Petra's ringing Col today.'

'Col at the Longhouse?' Wolfe pulls away from Tom excitedly.

'Just to see what the scene is there.'

'The Longhouse! We're going back to the Longhouse!' Wolfe dances around Tom's legs.

'Hey, mind my fish! Cool it a bit, mate, we don't know yet. To have the baby, probably, yes. Petra was really freaked at the idea of going into hospital last night. And once the baby's here we'll see. If it works out, if I fit in, then maybe yes. If not maybe a cottage somewhere near, or even a caravan. Not a word though,' Tom warns. 'I told Petra I wouldn't tell you, not till it's certain.'

Wolfe looks at the lovely strong salmon struggling upwards into the streaming water. He feels stupid because in his eyes are tears of relief and he keeps his head down to hide them from Tom. Through his tears the salmon looks more real than ever; it seems to wriggle and gleam.

*　　*　　*

Nell watches Petra with narrowed eyes. There she is, pegging the washing out all higgledy-piggledy on the line, and never a glance over, never a wave. She hasn't brushed her hair by the look of it – all greasy rats' tails – and she is outside in her slippers treading in all the ash from last night's fire which she will, no doubt, tread into her house, onto her sticky kitchen floor. Still, it was something last night to see the fireworks, a bit of a treat – and for all of them to see Olive making such a spectacle of herself. And it was something to witness the burning of the hat.

What Petra is doing stretching her arms up like that in her

condition, Nell doesn't know. And all those grubby-looking clothes. There is no order about it. The white things are greyish, the coloureds faded. These automatic washing machines are no progress at all, not if they make a muddle like that. Nell swears by her old twin-tub. Old faithful. Like a part of the family, Jim used to say, groaning and churning away in the kitchen, and though Nell never said, she quite agreed. She felt quite fond of the thing, if you can be fond of a machine. Though why she never said, she doesn't know. She tutted when Jim said things like that, jokey things, and sometimes she wonders now if she wasn't a bit tight-lipped with him, a bit on the stiff side. It wouldn't have hurt to laugh now and then when he made one of what he liked to think of as his jokes. Still, water under the bridge.

Nell's yellow rubber gloves reach her elbows. She is cleaning the insides of her windows, and later she'll get Rodney to get out the old ladder and do the outsides. He is still in bed, and Nell's face tightens as she wipes her wet leather over the windows, smearing Petra and her washing line into glittering suds. Rules are rules, after all, but what can she do? She knows what she ought to do and that's march into his room with a bucket of water and throw it over him. That would wake him up. Still in bed at ten o'clock indeed!

Petra goes back into the house. Nell screws a page of newspaper into a tight ball and goes over the window again, pressing so hard that the paper shrieks against the glass. But it is no good. Unless the outsides are done equally well, what is the point?

She goes upstairs and hesitates outside Rodney's room. All is quiet. She almost turns away, but then she knocks. She cannot be, will not be, afraid of her own son, in her own house. There is no answer. She turns the handle and pushes open the door. Rodney is in bed and he is reading. Nell cannot see, has no wish to see, precisely what it is that he covers up so quickly, so furtively. She does not wish to see or know, but she does know she can't have that sort of filth in her house. However.

'Are you thinking of getting up today?' she asks. 'Only we did talk about the windows after all the smoke last night.'

'In a bit, in a bit.' Rodney slumps back against his pillow and Nell lets her eyes wander round his room. His clothes and God knows what else are in heaps all over the floor. The curtains are drawn against the closed windows and it is dim and fusty. It smells like an animal's den.

'And once you're up I'll do your room out,' she says. 'You've got an appointment at the Job Centre this afternoon, don't forget.'

'Don't start at him,' he says. 'He's getting round to it.'

'Well see that you do,' Nell snaps. 'And see that you put those dirty things in the linen basket.' She goes out and closes the door. It is going to be difficult having Rodney here, a real trial. He is not under control, not properly. The house is not even under control now that he is in it. It was controllable when there was just her, just her own things to clean and tidy. In Nell's head there is a kind of intricate diagram, a grid, of the house and all its nooks and crannies, all the places dirt and grime collect, and she cannot rest if they are not patrolled regularly. When she was alone, that was easy – well, manageable. But now another body – and a big and grimy one at that – invades her space. She cannot be there every time he puts a cup down, every time he uses the lavatory, every time his outside shoe touches her floor. She cannot always be there with her wet cloth, and so she worries. It may be irrational. She suspects that the extent of her fear of dirt is irrational, but it cannot be helped. It is real, as real as the dirt, as real as the creatures that need the dirt to mate in.

No, she cannot always be there. It may be good to have Rodney there for appearances. She is not an old woman living alone any more, no longer the prey of thugs. And what a good mother, what a warm-hearted woman she must seem to be that he should choose to return to her. But it is not comfortable. Not with those children next door either, that sneaky little lad with his scabby skin and his shifty eyes. A constant reminder to Rodney. Although he is cured. Oh yes he is. They wouldn't have let him out, if he wasn't cured. They know what they are doing, the authorities. They must know what they are doing or wherever would we be?

But he has that temper still. When he was a small child it was easy enough to sort him out, a spell in the cupboard under the stairs, or perhaps, in the worst cases, in the cellar, always did the trick. He'd go in like a lion and come out meek as a lamb. That was easy enough, although she'd had to leave it to Jim when he got bigger and stronger. And she had to go on at Jim to get on with it, too soft by half, poor love. But now Jim is next to useless and Rodney is a full-grown man. He is taller and far heavier than Nell and if – God forbid – there was any question of a struggle . . . well . . .

Nell goes downstairs and fills her bucket with fresh water, with a great squirt of detergent to whip up into a foam, and then she lugs the bucket back upstairs and into her bedroom.

She gives Jim a quick going-over with a corner of her leather. 'There we are love,' she says, smiling fondly, 'that's you spick and span, at least.' Jim does not reply.

She goes to the window and loops back the net curtains. She balances on her dressing-table stool and starts on the front window. She rubs the clean bubbles over the glass, almost happy in her task for a moment, aware that Jim is watching her endeavours, seeing that she hasn't let things slip, enjoying the vigour of the task, the clean lemon smell of the detergent. And then she sees something that freezes her arm in mid-air, that makes her wobble on the stool and causes the blood to drain from her head so that her vision is clouded with blackness and she has to sit and place her head between her stiff nylon-clad knees.

From above, she has seen a hat. There it was, directly below her, a black hat with those cherries, those unmistakable cherries. That's all she saw, just the hat, there below her, just *the* hat. And now the blood surges and sings in her ears. She forces herself to stand up and look out of the window and, just in time, she sees a woman disappearing down the road wearing the hat. And she can't be absolutely sure, but she thinks that it is Petra.

* * *

Arthur stands on the boundary between his plot and Jim's. He's eased a few fine and creamy parsnips from the ground but there's nothing else he can do today, he hasn't the time. He can't leave Olive for long, and there's the cat to find, but he can stand and look. The full moon has worked its magic and the tiny furled heads of the bean shoots are just showing above the earth. He stands with his back to Jim's plot. He stands on the place where the boundary was changed. In his hand is the godstone, but he has the feeling he always has while standing on the boundary, that all is not well. It is not that Jim's plot has gone to rack and ruin, nor that his own is likely to follow suit as the years wear him down. It is not that. It is not as easy to put a finger on as that. It is simply an inkling that all is not well.

When the bombers flew low over the city on a brilliant moonlit night, they'd seen the glass from the greenhouses gleaming, and had rained their bombs down upon the allotments, splintering the glass, cracking the frosted winter earth and sending the parsnips and the Brussels sprouts flying. Jim had been away in Italy, fighting; Arthur had been in Norfolk, farming; and their plots had been smashed, churned, and had stayed like that until the spring when Jim, recovering

from a wound, came home for a few weeks' respite. He had
been the one who had picked the shards of glass from the
earth, pulled the weeds which had so greedily rooted themselves in the good soil, levelled it all off again – and redefined
the boundary. Arthur had never said a word because Jim had
worked so long and hard on his allotment for him. Arthur had
never asked Jim why he had moved the boundary – it must be
nearly a yard – and widened the turf path too, so that Arthur
had lost a good strip of his plot. He'd never said. How could he
without sounding petty, ungrateful? When he returned his plot
was dug and manured and planted, good as new. Jim was a
friend. Not a comrade, no, but on the allotment he was a
friend. There was that business with Olive that he took so
seriously. Olive had taken Jim for a lover on a whim, that was
all. It had soon been over, curiosity satisfied. It had been over
as far as Olive was concerned. It was only Jim, Olive told him,
who couldn't let the matter rest, talked about being 'in love',
wanted to divorce Nell and marry Olive! And Olive had had to
send him packing back to Nell with his tail between his legs.
Poor old sod.

Arthur picks up the tail of a rocket, flown from somewhere
last night and landed amongst his seedlings. He stirs the toe of
his boot in the moist soil and allows himself to imagine, just for
a moment, his own son as a man. This is his indulgence. The
lad had been dark with cloudy blue eyes; a wise and wizened
face; tiny, perfect. If he had lived, what would he have
become? A farmer? A craftsman? A politician? A doctor? He
might have been here now, with his old dad, helping on the
allotment, or driving the grandchildren over to see Olive. He
would have been a help with Olive.

But this is useless. He is nothing.

Before he was six weeks old, he died. One morning they had
slept late and woken to stillness and Olive had known. She had
leapt from the bed, clutching her leaking breasts, and she had

not cried out when she had found him cold and perfect in his
cot. She had just looked, just stood and looked, the front of her
nightdress darkening with wasted milk. She had just stood
there and looked, and Arthur had had to move her gently aside
to pick up his son and to be certain that the life had gone from
him.

There are tears in Arthur's eyes as he gazes at the green
sparks in the soil. Olive's grief had been a deep river in which
they had both nearly drowned. It had taken all his strength to
keep her up, save her from the swirling downcurrents of utter
despair. He had had no energy for his own grieving. The death
of his baby son left a space inside him, a dry space where a new
kind of tenderness had been growing. No other child had come
along to soften the memory of the tiny lad and now, anyway,
now he has someone to care for. He has Olive, and to Olive he
must return.

                         *   *   *

Nell draws back Rodney's curtains and flings open the
window so that she can breathe. Rodney has finally gone for
his interview, half an hour late, having failed to clean the
windows first. Nell will restore order to his room, if it's the last
thing she does.

And it is all right about the hat. It gave her a turn, all right,
bobbing along like that, large as life, when she thought it was
gone to ash and smoke, but it is not so strange really. Not when
you stop to think for a minute. They didn't burn it, that is all,
she must have been mistaken. In all the confusion of smoke
and flames she thought she saw it burning, an understandable
mistake. Petra must have taken a fancy to the hat and decided
to keep it. That is all. Nothing to get in a state about. But what
if Arthur sees it, what if Olive? She will just have to give it
back, that's all. A mistake, she'll say; Don't know what got

into me, she'll say. And they'll give it back, of course they will, why ever shouldn't they? And then she can decide what to do for the best with the wretched hat. She's beginning to wish she'd let it be, left it in the gutter, which was a fitting place for it after all. And she will keep herself under control. She will not get into a state over something as trivial as a hat. She will keep herself under control and get on with the matter in hand. Which is Rodney's room.

The balsa-wood aeroplanes sway in the breeze from the windows. Nell pauses for a moment, watching them, wondering where to start. She pulls on her rubber gloves before she picks up the foetid clothes, the socks stiff with dried sweat, and, holding her breath, she takes them out to the linen basket. She pulls back the candlewick bedspread which is crumpled now after years of smoothness, and the blankets, and shudders at the sight of the sheets, crumpled and dampish. There are unmentionable hairs too, and even biscuit crumbs, despite her rule about food in the bedroom. There is a cup of cold skinned-over coffee beside the bed, and hairs on the stained pillowslip. Her face is stony as she strips the bed and flaps and smooths the underblanket. The room needs a good vacuum and polish and what-have-you. Really and truly it needs fumigating.

If only Rodney would get a job so that he was out all day, things might be manageable. She might be able to get used to it. If only he was safely packed off every morning, then she could get in here first thing and then the dirt would not have time to gather, the dust to settle, the germs and the mites to breed. Before his return, the room had been a pleasure to enter, with all the toys in their places, even the books regularly taken out and dusted. She had kept the room like that just in case. Just in case what? Just in case it would all come right in the end, her boy come home to her again. But that was all codswallop, she can see that now, for her boy could never come home to her again. Her boy does not exist. How much more satisfactory the hope of Rodney's return had been than the fact of it. How much more satisfactory to see the smooth clean bed, the innocent toys and books waiting. And how terrible to have a middle-aged stranger besmirch her memories.

She pulls Mr Wog out from under the bed, and then she pulls out the magazines. She does not mean to look. She does not mean to do more than look at the price to see how much of his dole he's wasted on the filth. She does not mean to see. But somehow the pages turn. She does not wish to know that there are magazines like this. She thought it would be tarts. But it is worse than that. It is diabolical. It is obscene. It makes her skin crawl, her scalp prickle, a bitter gorge rise in her throat to think what has been going on while she slept clean in her bed only the thickness of a wall away. What has been going on in his head. She has to close her lips to keep herself from whimpering as the pages turn. When she has seen it all, seen every obscenity, when she knows it all, what it is that goes on in Rodney's head, she begins to rip them up. She tears the magazines into strips and then the strips into tiny scraps, into a pile of tiny scraps of skin-coloured confetti and she flushes them down the lavatory. She flushes and she flushes but they do not want to go, they float up, they will always float up, bob mockingly up through the bubbling water. When she's done what she can, she sits weakly on the edge of Rodney's bed, discovering that she's hardly breathed for minutes on end. Her eyes are contaminated with what she's seen. She is defiled. There is no way that she can clean her mind. Damn Rodney. Damn him to Hell. She tries to take a deep breath, but her diaphragm is stuck, inside she has turned to stone. Too many shocks in one day. Too many shocks. Rodney is a viper. He is an impostor. He is no longer her son. She will cast him out. She stands up. Fury roars through her arms and she takes every book and every toy from the shelves and hurls them out of the open window. She plucks the planes from the ceiling and sends them out too. She rips the curtains off their rails so that the hooks pop all over the room. And then with a bucket of water and a bottle of bleach she starts to scrub.

* * *

Petra is making a cake when Wolfe and Tom arrive home. 'Mum!' Wolfe says, and flings his arms around her back, laying his face against her, stretching his arms around her enormous girth.

'Goodness! What's all this in aid of?' Petra laughs. 'Had a nice day?'

'Great,' says Wolfe. 'Tom's picture was brilliant. It was a fish. We got lots of money, didn't we, Tom . . .'

'Well . . .' Tom wags his hand back and forth and grins at Petra.

'By the way, Wolfe,' Petra says, 'would you take the cat next door to Arthur's and see if it belongs to them? It's been terrorising Nothing all day. I shoved it out in the garden in the end, but it hasn't moved a muscle as far as I can see. I heard Olive out there earlier, calling, as if she was calling a cat. Would you go and see?'

Wolfe sticks his finger in the bowl of pale grainy cake mixture, and licks it.

'Oi,' Petra complains.

'All right then,' Wolfe says. 'I'll take it now.' He has to go away from Petra anyway because his face feels as if it will burst with the need to smile, because he will burst with not knowing what Col said to Petra, and not being able to ask. Behind Petra's back Tom lifts his eyebrows and puts his finger to his lips and Wolfe nods.

He goes outside again to find the cat, crouched pale and bony in the ashes. He is a little afraid of the cat and its knowing human eyes, and so he hesitates and looks around – and notices that the cat isn't the only strange thing in the garden. There is a balsa-wood aeroplane, nosedived into the weeds; there are some books on the ground with their pages flapping in the breeze, and there is an old black rag doll. He picks up the doll and then sees that there are even more things in Nell's garden. There are more books, and toy cars and a wooden lighthouse and several aeroplanes with their wings all smashed on the paving stones. He looks up and sees that the upstairs window is wide open, and then he jumps as Nell's gate bursts open and Rodney appears.

'What the hell?' Rodney shouts, and his face is red and bits of spit fly from his mouth with his voice. 'What the hell's going off here? Mr Wog!' he points to the doll.

'Is he yours?' Wolfe hastily passes him over the hedge and Rodney stuffs him under his arm. 'He was in my garden,' he explains.

Rodney is looking round the garden, looking at all the toys and books. 'Fucking mad,' he says, and his voice is a bit quieter, quite calm. 'His mother is a fucking nutter.'

'Whose mother?'

'He always knew it. And the way she goes on at him! He's had her up to here.' He puts his hands against his forehead. He smiles at Wolfe, and his lips are red and wet.

'Well, bye-bye,' Wolfe says nervously.

'No, wait,' Rodney stretches out his hand to Wolfe. Wolfe edges away and then immediately feels sorry. He feels sorry for the man with grey in his hair and the doll under his arm. Wolfe sees that he is trembling. He steps forward and lets Rodney's big hand knead his shoulder. 'You're a good lad, aren't you?' Rodney says. 'You're not afraid of him, are you?' Rodney lets go of Wolfe and takes off his glasses to rub his eyes. 'Are you?'

'Afraid of who?' asks Wolfe. He cannot bear to look at Rodney's naked eyes. 'No, course not,' he says.

'Will you come to the Cutlers' Wheel?'

'I can't today . . .'

'But you're not at school.'

'Eczema,' Wolfe says, holding out his hands.

Rodney puts his glasses back on and looks. 'Poor little hands,' he says. 'You'll come to the Cutlers' Wheel and see the water rushing? Then when you get back you can tell your mum, surprise your mum.'

'Well, I don't know. I can't now, I've got to take the cat back . . . and it'll be getting dark soon.'

'Not for a bit. He'll be waiting. Half an hour . . .'

'But my mum . . .'

'Half an hour.'

Wolfe wants to say no, would have said no, but Nell opens the back door at that moment.

'Rodney,' she calls, 'Rodney.'

'Half an hour,' Rodney mutters once more, as he turns away.

'Wolfe?' Petra opens their own door and looks out. 'What are you doing? Aren't you taking the cat?'

'Yes, but look . . .' Wolfe points to the toys and books strewn across the gardens and Petra comes carefully down the back steps, her hand under her belly as if she is holding it up.

'How peculiar,' she says. 'They must have been having a clear-out. Funny people,' she whispers, grimacing. She peers over the fence. 'But some of those things must be quite valuable – those cars are in good nick. And that Meccano. My brother used to have some of that. Fancy chucking it all out!'

Wolfe picks up the broken plane. 'What shall we do with them?'

'Chuck them back over, I should think.' Petra shakes her head. 'And they've got the window wide open too! They must be freezing in there. I'm going in.' She shivers. 'Are you taking the cat back then?'

'Yes . . .'

'And stay and talk for a bit won't you? I expect they like to see a young face now and again.'

'Yes I will . . . Mum?'

'What?'

'They're all right, the people next door, aren't they?' he points to Nell's house.

'Of course they are. Whatever do you mean?'

'You said they were funny. And Rodney seems a bit funny, he talks in a cupeliar way.'

'Peculiar,' corrects Petra, smiling. 'Well it takes all sorts,' she adds, climbing the steps. 'I shouldn't worry.'

'Mum?'

'What?'

'Oh nothing. See you later.'

''Bye love.' The back door closes and Wolfe sighs and turns back to the cat. He scoops it up. It feels sharp and fragile through its thin skin. He carries it carefully round the front and down the passage to Arthur's front door. The skin on its back is cold, but underneath, in the folds where its legs meet its body, it is warm. He can feel the speedy beating of its heart against his hands and see the blue and red squiggles of its veins. Its tail is like a bone snake, tiny bones getting tinier and tinier as they reach the minute lashing tip. He holds it tightly under one arm as he knocks on the door.

He has to wait a long time before the frosted glass darkens and the door is fumbled open, and then the cat struggles free and leaps into the house. Olive peers round the door at him.

'Is it yours?' Wolfe asks.

'Oh yes, he's mine.'

'He was in our garden.'

Olive looks closer. 'Oh it's little lad from next door is it? He's a daft bugger isn't he? In your garden, you say? Well, come in then, don't stand there letting the cold in.' She stands back and Wolfe squeezes round the edge of the door. It is dim inside, gloomier than it is outside. The lights are on but the bulbs are weak and everything is brown and cluttered.

'Come in and have a sweet,' Olive says. 'Little lads like sweets, don't they? Don't they?'

Wolfe nods. 'I do anyway,' he says. Olive leads him into the front room. She is huge in her sagging cardigan and her socks, and her hair stands up round her head in a yellowish frizz. She opens a cupboard and pulls out a tin. 'It's a long time since we had a little lad in the house,' she says, straining with the effort of taking the lid off the tin. 'Here we are . . . see what you can find in there.' She hands the tin to Wolfe. Inside is a half a bar of chocolate, some nutty toffee and some chocolate limes. Wolfe's eyes widen. 'Sit down then,' commands Olive, and he perches on the arm of a huge leather chair.

'Can I take bit of chocolate?'

'Whatever you like.'

'*And* a chocolate lime?'

Olive nods. Her mouth is full of toffee now, and she strokes Mao who has jumped on the chair and stretches up his head to her, purring loudly. For a moment Olive and Wolfe chew companionably, concentrating, passing the tin between them, listening to Mao's content and the occasional ping of the old gas fire. Olive screws her face up with the effort of swallowing a lump. 'And you found my Mao. In your garden you say?'

'Sitting in the bonfire ash.'

'He will have been scared.'

'Of the fireworks.'

'That's right, lad. A good lad. We had a lad once . . . but we never talk . . .' she drifts off. Wolfe helps himself to another chocolate lime.

'Is Arthur in?' he asks. 'Only I'd like to see Arthur.'

'He's out searching for Mao.'

'Oh dear,' says Wolfe. 'Shall I go out and find him? Shall I tell him that we've found him?'

'No, lad, you stay put. He'll be back in a bit. Have another sweet. Try a bit of toffee. He'll be back in a bit. It'll be a nice surprise.'

'All right.' Wolfe swallows his half-chewed chocolate lime and takes a piece of the toffee. 'Why is he a bald cat?' he asks.

'Don't you think he's nice?'

'Yes,' Wolfe says. 'Only I like them better with fur.'

Olive laughs and when she opens her mouth wide Wolfe can see a gap between her teeth and her gums. 'It's nice to have a lad in the house,' she says. 'Come here, help me get down.' She grasps Wolfe's arm but he can't hold her weight and she overbalances on the floor with him on top of her. He jumps up, terrified.

'Are you all right?'

'Oooh,' she groans. 'It's just my back, my blessed back.'

'Shall I go and get my mum?'

'No, no . . . it'll pass. Artie will be home in a bit.' The cat jumps onto her chest and nestles itself down. 'There we are, Mao,' Olive murmurs.

'That's an unusual name for a cat,' says Wolfe politely. 'Miaow.'

'Chairman Mao.'

'Chairman Miaow.'

'And what's your name again?'

'Wolfe.'

Olive begins to laugh, but it turns into a groan. 'Oh my blessed back. Fetch a cushion, Wolfe, and put it under my shoulder.' Wolfe looks around and finds a lumpy flowered cushion. He bends over Olive to ease it underneath her and is enveloped in a choking smell of toffee and something powdery and old. He straightens up and stands awkwardly, shifting from one leg to the other. He would like to go now, but doesn't feel that he can leave her like this. He will wait for Arthur. Besides, he wants to see Arthur.

'I've got my cat back then,' Olive says, 'but there's still my hat. I lost my hat, a grand hat it was, black straw, with cherries. Oh yes, a grand hat all right.' Wolfe frowns. 'A grand hat and they've stolen it, the thieving buggers. I'll never see that hat again.'

Wolfe is confused. He opens and then closes his mouth. He thinks of the hat in Petra's wardrobe. *That* is a black straw hat with cherries on it. But that came from Nell and not from Olive. Perhaps all old women have hats like that. Olive looks as if she is going to cry. It is very odd to be in a room with a fat old woman flat on her back and a bald cat curled on her chest. He wonders what he should do if she does cry, but it is all right. She suddenly lets out a long sigh like a lilo going down and smiles at him. All the little hairs around her mouth glisten with toffee juice, and her chin trembles.

'Our little lad was a lovely lad,' she says. Wolfe is grateful that the subject has been changed. He will have to think about the hat. Olive stares up at him until he feels uncomfortable, but her eyes are not focused on him. 'Not like that lad up road,' she says, 'Nell's son. Not like him. Do you know about him?'

'Rodney?'

'That's the one, you want to keep out of the way of him . . . yes, keep right out of the road of him . . .'

'But . . .' Wolfe begins, but the door bangs and Arthur comes in. Olive's voice drops to a whisper: 'They had to put him away for years and years.'

'Ollie!' says Arthur sharply, coming into the room. 'What are you saying? Don't go frightening lad.'

'I'm not,' Olive's voice is plaintive now. 'He's fetched our Mao back to us.'

'Oh . . . that's a right relief! I've been everywhere. Where was he?'

'In our garden, just sitting in our garden,' Wolfe says.

'Daft bugger,' Olive says. 'But he's home now.'

'Language,' says Arthur.

'It's all right,' Wolfe says, 'everyone swears in our house too, except Mum. She fell down,' he explains, indicating Olive, 'but she says she's all right and we've eaten loads of sweets.'

Arthur laughs. 'Just as well I've got more supplies in then.' He puts his hand in his pocket and brings out some wine gums and some peanut brittle. 'You take a few home with you, here . . .' He opens the packet and fills Wolfe's hands with them. 'And here, a reward,' he puts a fifty-pence piece in Wolfe's coat-pocket.

'Thanks a lot,' says Wolfe. 'But it was nothing, he was only in the garden.'

'All same, lad, you brought him back safe and sound, and I'm right grateful.'

'Well, I'd better be going,' Wolfe says, awkward again. 'Bye-bye Olive, bye-bye Miaow.' Arthur follows him to the door and opens it for him.

'Er . . . you know what Olive was saying about Rodney . . .' Wolfe begins.

'Oh you don't want to go taking any notice of her,' Arthur says cheerfully. 'You take it with a pinch of salt, lad.'

'All right, then,' says Wolfe. He is relieved, because Arthur must know.

He waits in the passage between his front door and Rodney's. He supposes that is where Rodney will look for him. It is cold and he has peanut brittle stuck between his teeth. He will wait for a little while, just a little while, for the afternoon is creeping past and it gets dark early these days, since the clocks went back. He can smell the sweet warmth of Petra's cake drifting down the passage. He wants to be in the house with Petra and Tom and all the happiness and all the excitement, eating cake and keeping warm, waiting for Petra's news. If he dares, when Rodney comes, he will say, 'No, not today.' If Rodney comes soon, for he won't wait long. It is cold in the passage and the wind blows leaves and a crackly crisp bag about his feet.

The shouting has stopped so maybe Rodney will be out in a minute. The shouting was terrible. It is terrible to hear grown-up voices raised like that. Petra never shouts like that, nor does Tom. Nell's voice was like a wild screeching, rising and rising, though he could not make out the words; and he could hear Rodney too, shouting and bellowing, and even sobbing. And there were thumping and crashing sounds, as if furniture was being moved about, knocked over, and the sound of breaking glass. Wolfe listened to that and he was frightened. At least they are quiet now. He will not wait much longer for Rodney. Surely Rodney will understand that he could not wait now that it is getting cold and dusky? But then he might be angry with Wolfe and Wolfe could not bear it if Rodney shouted at him like that, in that bellowing voice, loud enough to rattle the glass in the door.

It is very quiet now that the shouting has stopped. It is very quiet but for the scratching sound of the leaves and the crisp bag blowing about, and the faint murmur of the radio from his own house. They are listening to *Afternoon Theatre*, and the cosy smell of the cake is seeping out, calling to him. He keeps his eyes on the door, but there is no movement. He can't wait much longer. He will not. He shivers.

Bobby and Buffy arrive suddenly, their voices loud and familiar and quarrelsome, their school-bags slung over their shoulders.

'What are you hanging about there for?' Bobby asks.

'No reason,' says Wolfe.

'Come on in then,' Buffy says and opens the door. 'It's freezing.' Wolfe follows them into the warmth and the light, glad to have his mind made up for him, glad not to be walking with Rodney through the blowing leaves and into the nearly dark. Rodney might not be a proper stranger, but he is strange for a grown-up. Not like a proper grown-up at all in some ways. And his eyes without glasses are pale and frightened eyes, curled-up eyes, like woodlice when you lift a stone.

Petra smiles at Wolfe. 'There you are at last,' she says. 'I was wondering where you'd got to. We were just about to send a search party out, weren't we, Tom?'

'Were you?' Wolfe asks, comforted.

The cake sits on a plate in the middle of the table, a round cake dappled with fruit and nuts and sprinkled with brown sugar.

'Now that we're all here, I've got some news,' Petra says. Her eyes are sparkly and excited. 'Sit down, and I'll cut the cake.'

Tom is sitting at the table with a cigarette dangling from his smile. He winks at Wolfe, and Wolfe sits down beside him.

Petra begins to slice the cake, and a sweet steam rises from it into the air. Petra gives the first slice to Wolfe, and as he sinks his teeth into the warm and spicy sweetness, all the cold and worrisome thoughts of Rodney float right out of his head.

*   *   *

Nell sits bolt-upright on the edge of the sofa. The room is cold. She will switch the gas fire on soon. It is nearly six o'clock. She can switch the gas fire on when it is six o'clock. Her eyes are on the clock. Her vision bores a tunnel through the room, outside which all is blurred. She keeps the tunnel focused on the clock. Jim used to wind that clock before he went upstairs to bed every night, and Nell has kept up the tradition. It is a reliable clock and when it says six o'clock she will switch on the fire. In order to switch on the fire she will have to step over Rodney.

In the corner is the telephone. It has hardly been used since

Jim passed over. Some bills have only the rental charge on them. She means to have it disconnected. It is only another thing to dust. But now she could use it to ring for an ambulance. She could dial 999 – but that seems an awful fuss to make. It is best to keep this sort of thing within the walls of the house, no call to go making a performance of it. And the carpet will be a devil to clean. But no, she will not look down, not until six o'clock. Her own head is numb where Rodney grabbed her hair, and her face throbs where he struck her. And Rodney lies sprawled on the floor. It's a mercy Jim is upstairs. It would have upset him to see Rodney go for Nell like that. Insane. Like a wild beast, not her son, not a cherub of a baby with eyelashes long enough to make women sigh. A wild beast. And what was his reason? That she had cleaned his room! That she had taken the trouble to clear out all that old rubbish, all that old rubbish that meant nothing any more.

Now Rodney groans. 'Mum . . .' he says. But Nell will not look at him, not yet, great big baby, making such a fuss. Rodney groans again and is quiet. There is his breathing; there is the ticking of the clock; sometimes a car goes past; sometimes there is a voice or footsteps outside. Otherwise it is quiet.

She should scrub the carpet now, while the blood is still wet. Then she might get away without a stain. That is the only solution, otherwise it will be ruined and she'll never afford another of this quality. Jim always insisted on the best – one hundred per cent pure virgin wool, none of your poly-propelene for them. She must do it. It would be plain wicked to sit there and let the blood dry and ruin her carpet for ever, a wicked waste. And anyway it is six o'clock, time to move.

She focuses her eyes on Rodney and it looks as if the blood is thickening on his head. That is good – no use cleaning while it's still flowing. She stands up and her own head hurts as she moves and she knows she must look a fright, and there is blood on her apron too, and on her cardigan. She dithers for a minute, unsure where to start. She goes to the airing cupboard and finds an old sheet which she folds into a pad, and then, to be quite sure, backs with a polythene bag. She tries to roll Rodney over with her foot. It is difficult, for he is heavy and struggles clumsily against her, and she has to kneel down eventually and use both hands and all her strength to roll him away from the sticky patch on the carpet. She puts the padded sheet under his head to prevent any more damage.

In the bathroom she takes off her blood-stained clothes and puts them to soak in a bath of cold water. Cold water is quite sufficient to lift blood out of clothes, so long as it isn't allowed to dry. She puts on her housecoat and her rubber gloves. She fills a bucket with water and detergent. She takes a scrubbing brush and a sponge, and then she sets to work. Once she is scrubbing it is all right. The important thing is to save the carpet. It keeps her warm, working so hard, and there is not even any need to switch on the fire after all that, and that will save on the bill. But the important thing is to save the carpet. Never mind about tea, tea can come later. Rodney will probably turn his nose up at it anyway. Poached eggs she'd thought. But no, eggs are not safe any more. Welsh rabbit then, with a splash of Lea and Perrins. Two slices, for this is hard and hungry work. Her stomach rumbles at the thought, a cold mechanical sound. She has a good technique: first she scrubs a patch of the carpet with detergent until there is a vivid pink foam and then she sponges it up and squeezes the sponge into the bucket. It is coming up a treat. She'll scrub the whole stain and then fetch clean water and go over it again and again until eventually the foam remains white, and the carpet is clean.

The redness reminds her of the cochineal she used to use to make pink icing for birthday cakes. She remembers a birthday party when she was a child, her own party. In the centre of the table there had been a pink and silver cake, a great glamorous mountain of a cake, and everyone had sung to her and raised their glasses. And she made cakes like that for Rodney every year, wanting him to have happy memories, beating the cochineal into the butter icing until it was the most delicate shade of pink. Perhaps it would have been better if she'd had a girl. Perhaps she could have managed a girl. She always iced birthday cakes with pink, until she learnt that cochineal was made of crushed-up beetles' wings. And anyway, there's been no call for birthday cakes, not for donkey's years.

'Mum,' says Rodney suddenly, bringing her back to the moment with a start. She'd almost forgotten he was there.

'Don't fuss,' gasps Nell. The scrubbing is hard, it makes her breathless. 'I'll just get this done and then I'll see to tea.' Her head is beginning to throb in earnest now. The claws are tightening again. And maybe it was wrong of her to throw the iron at Rodney like that when he came at her like a wild beast. Maybe it was wrong, but she didn't mean any harm. She didn't mean *such* harm.

'I think it's time you went to bed.' Nell leans over Rodney and pokes him with her toe. 'You can't lie about there all night like a spare part. And you've let your tea get cold. Come on.' She kneels beside him and lugs him up into a sitting position. The cut on his head has stopped bleeding although it gapes still and his hair is clotted with big blobs of blood, shiny as blackcurrants.

'Can't,' murmurs Rodney.

'No such word,' Nell says. 'Now come on, set your mind to it. Turn over onto your hands and knees . . .' She half shoves, half helps him over. 'Good,' she encourages. 'That's very good, see, you can do it if you try.' She picks up his glasses and rubs them with her apron. 'Now, crawl to the stairs.' She stands behind him, her arms folded, watching him inch precariously forward. 'A bit further,' she says. It feels all right

with him down on his hands and knees, a harmless baby. She
feels better about him as she follows him along, urges him up
the stairs and into his cold clean room.

'I had to do it,' she says, closing the window. 'There was so
much rubbish, so much old junk. Mites can live on anything,
you know, and worms eat through the pages of books. Don't
know what I was thinking of, harbouring such rubbish.' She
refrains from thinking about the rubbish still floating in the
toilet. 'Dustbin day tomorrow,' she says. 'First thing I'll get out
and get that lot bagged up.' She looks out into the dark garden
where the page of a book flaps feebly to and fro in the light
from the window.

The bed is in the middle of the floor and there is nothing else.
The curtains have gone and the rug, and the bookshelves are
bare. One cupboard stands empty, its door open. The room
smells of bleach. 'It's all right now,' Nell says comfortingly,
looking round. She helps Rodney heave himself onto the bed.
He is the only unclean thing in the room. His jacket and shirt
are bloody. He must be washed, she realises, looking un-
happily at his trousers, undressed and washed – but that can
wait till morning. Her head will stand no more tonight. She
puts the pad of sheet under his head to stop him soiling the
pillow, takes off his shoes, covers him with a blanket and tucks
his glasses under the pillow.

'God bless,' she says and the words dislodge a memory.
There was a lullaby she used to sing. She hums feebly for a
moment until the words come back, and her voice
vibrates through the coldness, a high mosquito whine:

'Wink and Blink and a Nod, one night,
Sailed off in a wooden shoe,
Over a river of crystal light
And into a sea of blue.

' "Where are you going and what do you wish?"
The old man asked the three.

"We're going to fish for the herring fish,
That live in the beautiful sea." '

Rodney's face twitches once, as if he is puzzled, and then he is still. 'God Bless, my cherub,' she whispers and she goes out, closing the door silently behind her, for her baby is sleeping, as peacefully as ever.

'What's been going off?' asks Jim the moment she enters the bedroom, 'all that banging and shouting.'

'Nothing, 'love,' Nell says, undressing beneath her nightdress, 'nothing to worry yourself over.' She touches his frame with her fingertips. 'God bless,' she says and then, without warning, flips him onto his face, for she is in no mood for his fretting tonight.

Her head is heavy on the cool pillow and she arranges her arms outside the bedspread to keep herself from overheating. Her head throbs, the soft coldness blotting the pain like lint. In the mirror she has seen the bruise on her cheek. She will look a proper sight tomorrow.

It takes her a long time to get off to sleep. The thought of the cherry hat will not go away. She meant to go next door and ask Petra for it back, but how could she in all the kerfuffle? It is only a stupid hat, a thing, anyway. What does it matter what becomes of it? She knows all that but the thought of it will not leave her alone. When she closes her eyes she sees Olive in the hat, her lips as red as the cherries, her eyes blacker than the straw. Her eyes are bright and dancing, looking into Jim's. Oh yes, Nell is not so naïve that she didn't notice the fancy Olive took to Jim. Not content with one man, the alley cat. Lucky that Jim was the faithful type – not that he wasn't flattered. Perhaps he was even tempted momentarily by Olive's flashy charms, she can accept that. And to look at Olive now . . . if only Father *could* see how his little Gyspy had turned out.

Nell's face, blank in the dark, eyelids closed like lids of

stone, tries to smile, but there is something niggling, something else other than the hat, other than Rodney, something wriggling almost like a worm in her mind, something she cannot identify. She cannot put her finger on it, but it is to do with Olive, something to do with Olive.

Eventually she drifts into a troubled sleep, and in her sleep she dreams. In her dream she holds the cherry hat and Olive, the young Olive, beautiful in a white dress with a blood-stain down the front, tries to take it but she cannot. Somehow she cannot, her hand goes right through it and Nell holds tight and she feels a power, shocking, like a blast of warmth, that wakes her. In another snatch of dream, Olive is old and she is wearing something on her head, something mad, but Nell cannot quite see what it is. She has to get closer to look, walk across stepping stones, walk across stepping stones to Jim's allot-ment, and there is Olive sitting outside his shed. And even though she knows in the dream that he is dead, he is still there, inside the shed, making something. She can hear him hammer-ing and sawing. And when Nell gets close to Olive she can see that she is laughing, and her hair is thick and black again, and on her head is balanced the silver cup, the school prize.

Nell wakes suddenly and sits up in bed, suffering with her head, feeling sick. The cup. She stole Olive's cup and she stole Olive's hat and now Olive is poor and fat and ridiculous. And oh how things seem different in the dark of night. She climbs out of bed and she has to use the lavatory and there are the coloured fragments bobbing in the water, the fragments that will not flush away. Nell goes back into her room and switches on the light. She stands Jim up.

'All right, love?' he says.

'The hat isn't burnt. I thought the children next door would have burnt it but they didn't.'

'That's good, isn't it?' Jim says, squinting at her through the old sunshine.

'I was thinking, dreaming about the cup. I didn't steal it, not really, Jim, you know I didn't. I found it, on the night of the Blitz when their house was hit. Things were thrown everywhere and in the morning I found the cup in our garden. It was filthy and I picked it up and polished it and I meant to give it back. I did. I always meant to give it back . . . but it was a difficult time, Jim, with you away and Rodney just a baby. I put it away in the sideboard, well you know, you found it there and I never got round, well I forgot all about it. After all it was a silly gimcrack really, wasn't it, Jim? Wasn't it? Not worth worrying about.'

'Important enough for me to bury.'

'Well I couldn't give it back then, could I? Not all that time later. She didn't need it. I don't suppose she gave it a thought. I don't suppose she missed it. She has everything. Olive. Wonderful Olive . . . deserved what she got, her poor bastard . . .'

'Her baby, Nell, her infant.'

'And she . . .' but Nell cannot think now where her bitterness has gone. She is shivering. 'No,' she says, and there is a tremor in her throat, an odd fluttering, 'she did not, after all, deserve that.' She switches off the light and climbs heavily back into bed and the slight warmth she's left there.

'Sleep now, my love,' says Jim.

'Yes,' Nell says. She lies flat on her back as usual, but unusually, tears trickle down the sides of her face. Olive is not to be envied. Perhaps she never was. Olive has not got everything, never had everything. She has not got a child. She has old Arthur, of course, but he is no man, not like Jim, he is more a lap-dog, foolish and devoted. She does not sleep again until the milky dawn seeps round the edges of the curtains.

Ten

Rodney is dead. Nell stands looking at him for a few minutes, puts out her finger, and touches his cheek. It is perfectly cold. His eyes, fortunately, are closed. 'That's that then,' she says. In death, she can see a trace of the boy Rodney, a trace even of Jim in the set of his lips, or perhaps it is her father. 'Good,' she says, and shocks herself. But it is true. It is good. It will save a lot of trouble.

Downstairs, she sits at the kitchen table and eats her All-Bran and sips her cup of tea. She feels that a weight has been lifted from her shoulders, they feel as light and fluttery as if she is sprouting wings. The beast-claws have loosened from her head and she feels clear and light. Almost light-hearted. But, of course, there is the problem of the body. Corpses are far from hygienic. Bodies are full of bacteria, live bodies that is, that are there from the moment of birth, from before birth even, lying dormant, like time bombs, waiting only for the moment of death to begin their repulsive life cycle, devouring the body from within as they spawn, making it fizz, ferment, explode. Nell read this somewhere and it has been with her ever since, just like the bacteria in her own body. And here she is with a corpse on her hands, in her Rodney's bed. All she knows for certain is that the eyes should be closed with coins. After breakfast she visits the corpse and places a shiny ten-pence piece on each of its eyelids. She does not undress and wash it yet; that must wait until she has the time to be thorough. She does tuck a white sheet neatly around it, but she does not cover its face like they do in the films.

If she called an undertaker, questions would be asked, would be sure to be asked. Doctors might be consulted, even the police dragged in about the gash on its head. But she has done nothing wrong. It was self-defence was the iron, and anyway, Rodney was her son. She gave him life, and she took it away. What could be fairer than that?

In the weeks before Rodney was born, she had knitted a shawl. It was a huge complicated affair in fine white wool, a great insubstantial cobweb of a thing, but warm. A most excellent shawl. The first time she had held Rodney swathed in the shawl he had seemed to weigh almost nothing in her arms. He was such a tiny boy, but strong, and he would wave his hands about and catch the little shrimps of his fingers in the net of the shawl and wail until she freed them, and smoothed and wrapped him again into a neat soft parcel. She flinches against the remembered tenderness rising like a forgotten taste in her throat. For a moment she is almost lost. She darts her eyes around the bare bright room as if for the first time. She remembers the warm shadowy folds of the shawl and the woolly tenderness. She stands on the chilly floorboards and for a second she is caught between the two things: the warm shadows and the bare brightness; the one too far distant, too long lost, and the other too terrible to contemplate. She wavers between them for an awful elastic second and then she snaps out of it, back into the present.

'Don't go having a turn, now,' she scolds herself. 'You've things to do.'

It is as well that it is not May or June, but November with a hint of frost in the air. She can see her breath, a clean white cloud in front of her. She opens the window wide. At this time of year, the back of the house gets no sun at all. The corpse will keep till later, at least until she has dealt with her more pressing business this morning. Nell frowns as she folds away the woollen blankets. They will have to be laundered before they can be used again. And the precious blue candlewick will need a wash too, and then, when the bed is vacated once more, it can lie flat again upon the empty bed, smooth and perfectly flat.

She washes her hands, scrubs them with a brush dipped in Dettol. She scrubs till her fingertips are sore and withered. What's done is done and she won't start dithering now. She will think positive. She will be able to regain control. No one else will ever set foot inside the house again while she has a say in it, and she will get it clean. If she has to work night and day, she will make it safe. It's a long time, too long, since she's pulled out the oven or the refrigerator, to clean behind. A heavy job. Pity she didn't get Rodney to do that. In the bathroom mirror she sees her face, an awful sight, the bruise on her cheek an angry swelling. Once that has faded, she will make an appointment for a perm. Her curls are getting loose and wild.

She bares her teeth in an ivory smile, for today she has good to do, amends to make. The wriggling worm in her mind is good. It is a clean and golden worm, not a nasty thing, and she is satisfied because she has worked out what it is. It is the larval form of her conscience. Poor old Olive Owens. Poor old bag. Poor fat old geriatric hag. They are in the same boat now – bereft of child – but at least Nell still has her faculties, her faculties *and* her figure. Olive does have Arthur, of course, but still . . . Nell had a terrible night, last night, what with the dreams and all, but she has woken up fired with a new resolve. She has heart enough in her thin breast to feel pity for Olive now, not sorrow, quite – for Olive at least partly deserves her condition – but pity certainly. And if she makes peace with Olive then there is always Arthur. He is a man of a sort, at least, and could perhaps be a help. He might, for instance, move the bins; and there's the kitchen window smashed by Rodney in his tantrum. Perhaps he might see to getting that mended.

Would Olive mind? she wonders. Would Olive be foolishly

jealous? For the shoe is on the other foot now. It is Nell who is the sprightliest. Yes, she'll have a perm as soon as she can. And perhaps she and Arthur can be a comfort to each other, once she makes her peace. For no one likes to be entirely alone.

*   *   *

Olive sits up in bed with a shawl around her shoulders. She sips the tea Arthur has brought her.

'I'm stopping here today,' she mumbles.

'Not feeling poorly, are you?' Arthur asks. He looks closely at her crumpled face.

'Can't be arsed to move,' Olive says, and Arthur winces. Olive's language gets worse as she gets older. It is as if bad language is easier than any other, that it slips in effortlessly when her brain is only half engaged.

'No need, Ollie,' he says. 'Eat your breakfast . . . here's your teeth.' She puts them in, and Arthur is relieved to see her face regain some structure. His own dentures are giving him gyp and he juts them forward in order to run his tongue round his sore gums.

'Pee,' Olive says plaintively. He helps her swing her heavy legs out of bed and onto the floor. Her feet and ankles are swollen and when she puts her weight on them they are pressed flat and yellow-white around the edges. Arthur follows her into the bathroom. While she sits on the toilet he runs a basin full of water for her to wash in. He looks at himself in the steamy square of mirror above the basin. His eyebrows are crags over his weak eyes. The rest of his face is shrunk to the shape of his skull, the skin brown and wrinkled as leather. He is not sorry to be old, and when he stirs the earth at the allotment with the toe of his boot he knows that he is not afraid to die. He runs his finger through the condensation on the mirror, leaving a trickling trail. It's just a waste that it didn't turn out better, his life, that he never did the things he said he'd do. After the war, somehow, they got stuck here, Arthur and Olive, despisers of private property, in the house that Olive had inherited from her parents. And he had worked. He had felt proud to be a worker and he had worked his best years in a steel mill and he and the mill had run down together, so that his retirement was a petering-out rather than an occasion. And it had all gone in a flash. And now he is old, and Olive is old.

'All right?' he asks. 'Are you done?' Olive nods and he helps her up. 'We'll just get you freshened up,' he says, wringing out a flannel in the hot water. 'How're your knees?' He looks at the wide flat scabs. 'Healing fine. I'll clip your toenails later.'

'Nails,' says Olive. 'Come on then, Arthur, play. Nails.'

'Hammer.'

'Sickle.'

'Hay.'

'Loft.'

'Roof.'

'Bomb.'

'Bomb?'

'Our roof, in war.'

'Sky . . . fell from.'

'Sunshine.'

'Summer.'

'Wine . . . Remember that summer, Artie? With the motor bike and the side-car. We went to Devon that summer, and the verges were all lacy with that stuff . . .'

'Cow-parsley.'

'Oh the awful summery stench of it! And the poppies in the fields. Remember the cream? Strawberry jam and scones and clotted cream.'

Arthur wipes her face. 'Let's get you back to bed,' he says. 'You want to drink your tea before it gets cold.'

He straightens the sheets and pulls down her nightie and arranges her comfortably against her pillows. Mao jumps up and snuggles beside her, purring at full volume. 'Yes, it were good in Devon,' he agrees.

'It's all been good. We've been happy, haven't we, Artie? Haven't we?'

'We have that, Ollie.' Arthur watches her chew her bread and marmalade.

'And I was beautiful, wasn't I, Artie?'

'You were, Ollie, and I were right lucky.'

'And sexy. I could have had anyone, Artie, you know, anyone, not just *her* Jim.'

Arthur sighs and nods.

'Not just him, no, I could have had anyone. Baden Powell, I could have had him, or Winston Churchill . . . never fancied him, but he wrote to me, you know, begging . . . Or Omar Sharif . . .'

'And I was the lucky one,' says Arthur warily. He is afraid that Olive's temper will surface now, for that is the pattern. First the memories then the fury – but this morning, so far, she is calm. He will not push his luck yet, he will not say he's off to the allotment later on, not yet.

'I'll get pots washed,' he says, when she's finished her breakfast, and he takes her cup and plate downstairs and all is quiet. He breathes a heavy sigh of relief.

*   *   *

Already there are boxes everywhere. In only a morning the house has been transformed from a home to just a building, a shell that they are leaving. The curtains and blinds have all been taken down so that the rooms look unusually bare and bright and scruffy in the frosty sunshine.

Wolfe's job is to take the books off the shelves in the front room and pack them into small cardboard boxes. It's no good packing them into big boxes, Petra explained, because big boxes full of books are impossible to lift. He's filled two and a half boxes and has got the sneezes from the dust that floats off the books as he pulls them out. His fingers itch too, and he pinches and squeezes the skin between them with his finger and thumb in an effort not to scratch. He wanders to the window to press his knuckles against the cold glass, and gazes out at the road, at the identical terrace of houses opposite. He does feel sad, just a bit sad, to be leaving this house. Not sad enough to cry, or even to mention it, but he has a dull feeling inside him as if something heavy is tied to his ribs, dragging him down. He thinks guiltily of Rodney. They will never have their trip to the Cutlers' Wheel now. He doesn't mind that for himself, but there are a few things he does mind leaving, that he will miss. One of them is his own room, with his own door to shut behind him at night. And another is Arthur – and Olive too. He likes Olive and there is something good he can do before he leaves; one thing he can do to make her happy. He goes upstairs to Petra's room. She is up in the attic sorting Bobby and Buffy out. All her clothes are sprawled on the bed. The floor is covered with coat-hangers and shoes and tights and socks and knickers. The wardrobe is empty – almost. He pulls up a chair and climbs up to reach the high shelf at the top. The hat is there, and he stretches up and reaches it down.

Wolfe knocks at the door and this time it is opened almost immediately, and by Arthur.

'Morning,' Arthur says.

'Hello,' Wolfe replies. He feels shy, standing there, holding behind his back a carrier bag with the cherry hat inside. Arthur looks at him expectantly.

'Do you want somat in particular, lad?' Arthur asks.

'I've got a present for Olive,' Wolfe says.

'Grand,' Arthur says. 'She'll be right pleased. She needs somat to buck her up this morning.' He lets Wolfe into the house. 'You go up, and I'll follow in a bit. Front bedroom. Can't miss it.'

Wolfe goes up. It is dim and chilly on the stairs and the old brown wallpaper is covered with snarling flowers. There is a fusty smell like jumble sales and old cupboards. The bedroom door is open and he peers round. 'Hello,' he says.

Olive frowns at him for a moment and then her face caves into a smile. 'It's little lad!' she says delightedly. 'Have you come to visit me? Here sit down on bed. Arthur! Arthur! Bring us sweet tin upstairs . . .'

Wolfe smiles and settles himself on the edge of the bed. 'How are you?' he asks, in the way Petra would.

'Little lad who brought Mao back to me . . . There he is, happy as Larry.' She indicates the sleeping cat, whose skin is quite pink in the warmth. 'Oh it's a long time since we had a little lad in house . . .' she sighs. 'We had a little lad once, but we don't talk . . . Arthur!' she calls again. 'Sweets.'

Wolfe likes the way she says the same things over and over. 'He'll be up in a minute,' he explains. 'He told me to come upstairs first because I've brought you a present.'

'Present? What present? Not Christmas is it?'

'No, I just thought you'd like it . . .'

'I love presents. Always loved presents, yes I'll like it I dare say . . .' Olive stretches out her hand and Wolfe gives her the bag. She grabs it and rustles inside, greedy and urgent as a child – and pulls out the hat. 'Artie!' she screams, and Mao wakes and shoots off the bed like a bullet. Wolfe is quite startled himself, and jumps up. Arthur comes hurrying creakily upstairs with the sweet tin. 'Look Artie! It's my hat! It's my cherry hat!'

'Well I'll be blowed,' Arthur says, standing in the doorway.

'Give him a sweet!' cries Olive cramming the hat onto her head, 'Oh there there, it's all right now . . .'

'Quieten down, Ollie,' smiles Arthur, 'you're scaring lad, and look at Mao.' The cat is flattened against the wall in a fierce arch.

'Where'd you get it?' Arthur asks.

'Chocolate,' Olive says. 'Give the lad some chocolate, Artie.' He opens the tin and Wolfe breaks himself off a square of fruit and nut. Olive fills her mouth too, and for a moment she is quiet.

'My mum had it,' Wolfe explains, 'but it wasn't really hers. I don't think it's yours either.' He looks at Olive.

'Rubbish,' she mumbles through her mouthful.

'Well it came from the other lady – Nell. She gave it to us for Bonfire Night.'

'Buggering bitch!' Olive exclaims, chocolate dribble escaping from her mouth.

'Language . . .' warns Arthur. 'I don't understand how . . .'

'Buggering thieving bitch,' Ollie says. 'Sod her. Fetch me a mirror, lad.'

'On dresser,' Arthur says.

On the dressing table, Wolfe finds a small hand-mirror with a pattern of pansies on the back. It is dusty so he wipes it on his sleeve before he hands it to Olive. She peers at her reflection for several moments, the cherry hat askew, a brown chocolate-ringed smile upon her face.

Arthur winks at Wolfe, or perhaps it is just a twitch, and Wolfe looks around the room at all the pictures on the walls, pictures of people waving banners and marching, lots of pictures of a pretty woman like a film star, a painting of a volcano.

'We're moving,' Wolfe announces, suddenly. 'Part of why I've come is to say goodbye.'

'Moving?'

'Going back home, to the Longhouse where we came from.'

'Didn't realise it was fixed up. Your mum never said,' Arthur says.

'We only decided yesterday . . .'

'And when are you off?'

'Tonight if we're ready. Tom's borrowing a van.'

'That's quick isn't it?' says Olive.

'It's because Mum's baby is coming soon. She wants to have it there. It's a commune and I was born there,' he finishes proudly.

'That's what Artie wanted, to live in a, whatsit, in a community.'

'Why didn't you then?' Wolfe asks.

Arthur shrugs.

'He lost heart after lad,' Olive says.

Arthur looks at her so sadly that it brings a lump to Wolfe's throat. He does not know what to say, but he clears his throat and tries. 'I'm sorry about the lad,' he says, 'but maybe you could come and visit us at the Longhouse. People do visit.' Arthur tries to smile, but this only makes him look sadder.

'Well, I'd better go,' Wolfe says. 'I didn't tell Mum I was coming round, and I've got to pack the books.'

'Have another sweet before you go,' Olive says. Wolfe is beginning to feel sick, but he takes a toffee and puts it in his pocket.

He smiles at Olive. 'Well, bye-bye then. You look very nice in the hat,' he adds, truthfully.

Arthur opens the door for Wolfe and he steps outside. 'Just a minute,' Arthur says. 'Here,' he reaches in his pocket for a pound coin, and pulls out the godstone too. He opens his palm to Wolfe. Wolfe almost picks up the coin, but then hesitates, his fingers poised over the stone.

'That's a nice stone,' he says. 'Can I look at it?'

'Take it,' Arthur says.

Wolfe holds it in his palm. It feels warm and special and friendly. It is like a little piece of Arthur, broken off and clean and white and warm. 'It feels like . . . magic . . .' he breathes.

'You take it then, keep it safe.'

'I can't.'

'I'll tell you story of stone,' Arthur says. 'It were in war, I didn't fight in war, refused . . . conscientious objectors they called us, and those of us that weren't locked up did different kinds of work. Well I worked on land. Best years of my life if only I'd known . . . one of my mates there were an old fella, Bill his name were. He give me the stone one day, told me it were his father's and maybe his father's before him, but Bill hadn't had no kids and so he gave it me. I've had it in my pocket ever since and that were . . . nearly fifty year back.' Arthur's voice is wavery, his pale eyes watery and far away.

'You can't give it to me! Not if you've had it all that time,' Wolfe says, but his fist has closed round the stone all the same, and he doesn't want to let it go. He wants to take it with him to the Longhouse, because holding it in his hand will be like holding Arthur's hand.

'Take it, please,' Arthur says. 'It's a gardener's godstone. A talisman. You hold it in your hand after you've set seeds and wish them strength – and just see how they grow.'

Wolfe pauses. 'Well, I am going to plant an apple tree at the Longhouse,' he says.

'There you are then, you'd best take stone.' Arthur clasps Wolfe's fist in his hand and gives it a squeeze.

'Thank you,' Wolfe says. He pauses. He'd like to ask about the lad, but doesn't dare. It is something terrible. It must be something terrible to make Arthur look so sad. 'If there's a war when I'm grown-up,' he says, 'I'll be a conscientious objector too, like you.'

'You get off now,' Arthur says, quite brusquely, and closes the door. Wolfe stands outside for a moment, disappointed by the farewell, puzzled by Arthur's sudden change of tone. He has not even promised to visit. But the godstone is warm in his hand, and he has work to do. He goes back home, his brow wrinkled in a frown. Grown-ups can be so odd. But at least Olive is happy about the hat.

*   *   *

The taxi drops Nell off on the road at the top of the allotments. She is bright with good intentions. The first part of her plan might have gone puzzlingly wrong but she will carry on regardless. She went next door this morning to ask for the hat back, and was surprised to find them packing up ready to leave. It seems a funny way to go on. Only been there a few months and flitting already, a fly-by-night job by the look of it and her looking fit to drop that baby any minute. And she couldn't find the hat, or said she couldn't. She did admit to having it, and even wearing it, just once, 'Just trying it for size,' she had said, having the grace to look a bit embarrassed. She looked for it, or pretended to look, but there was no sign – no wonder in all that mess and muddle. So that is that as far as the hat is concerned. And that is all right because if they are moving and if they take it away to Suffolk or wherever it is they're going then at least there's no danger of Arthur or Olive seeing it about. So that is all right. But the second part of her plan she is determined to carry out.

It is awkward lumping Jim's fork and spade along, with her handbag bumping against her side and all, but Nell is not complaining. She has work to do. It was the dreams that nudged her this way, her dreams and Jim. He is in her handbag now, jolting against her thigh, and he will have a nice surprise when she gets him out on the allotment. And she will dig with his spade, she knows the place. She remembers Jim setting the turf over the place where, after the war, after he'd discovered it in the back of the sideboard drawer, he'd buried the cup for her.

'OLIVE OWENS,' he'd read. 'EXCELLENCE. What are you doing with it, Nellie?' And she'd had to explain, shamefaced, red-faced, that it was only to keep it safe that she'd picked the cup up, and only out of kindness that she'd polished it – for Olive had never bothered and it was dull and tarnished – and it was only forgetfulness that kept her from giving it back. 'It's gone for good now as far as she's concerned,' she begged Jim. 'She doesn't care. She's more than likely forgotten all about it. It never mattered to her, not really. And I can't give it back now, it would look . . . it would look as if . . .'

'Hmmm,' he'd said and given her a very sideways look. 'Well you can't keep it either,' he'd said. And when he'd gone up to the allotment to sort out the bomb damage he'd taken it and buried it, with some other rubbish. He hadn't even had to dig a hole. The bomb had fallen between the two allotments and Jim had simply put the things in the hole and turfed over the lot so that it would never be disturbed.

And now Olive will have it back. A peace offering. Of course, Nell doesn't expect a civil word from the poor creature, but that is not the point. The point is the thing that niggles, pity or conscience or whatever it really is. The return of the cup should still it.

*   *   *

The books are all packed in the boxes and neatly stacked. Wolfe stands at the window, his breath misting a little circle in front of his face. The godstone is warm in his hand. He has shown it to no one. It will be his secret and he will use it on the Longhouse garden and they will be amazed at the greenness of his fingers, and one day when he is as old and craggy as Arthur he will pass it on to some other boy or girl.

The house is quiet. Petra and Buffy are upstairs finishing off the bedrooms and Tom and Bobby have gone to collect the moving van and fill it with petrol and oil. Wolfe can hardly believe the speed at which things are happening. Important things, grown-up things like moving house, usually take for ever, weeks and weeks at the very least. But they are going already, in just a few hours they will be gone. And tonight they will sleep at the Longhouse. Tom will come back and finish off. They cannot pack everything in one day, but Petra doesn't want to risk another night, she says, because she has had something called a show. It couldn't have been much of one for Wolfe didn't notice a thing, but it means that the baby is certainly coming soon. And that means Wolfe will be a big brother.

As he gazes out of the window, he sees Arthur go off, his cap pulled down over his eyes, his baggy trousers flapping round his thin legs. Wolfe bangs on the window and Arthur removes his hand from his pocket and raises it in greeting: no smile, just a grown-up nod of the head. Wolfe, with the warm stone in his hand, does the same.

He is about to wander off, go upstairs and see if he can help Petra, when he notices Kropotkin running out into the road. Wolfe watches him dart stupidly about, and stop right in the middle of the road wagging his stumpy tail. 'Mum!' he calls, 'Arthur's dog is out.'

'Never mind,' calls Petra.

'But he shouldn't be!'

'He'll be all right.'

'Mind your own business,' calls Buffy from the attic.

Kropotkin looks at Wolfe through the glass. He puts his head on one side and barks. Wolfe goes outside. Petra and Buffy are wrong. He knows that the dog is never allowed outside like that. He'll get run over scampering about in the road. Arthur would never allow him out like that. He goes out the front.

'Potkins!' he calls. Kropotkin looks at him and barks.

'Come on, Potkins.' The dog charges towards him, and Wolfe tries to catch his collar and misses. He goes half-way down the passage between his house and Nell's – so that at least the dog will be off the road – and calls again. Kropotkin, his mouth frothing with excitement, dives down the passage, almost bowling Wolfe from his feet. He plunges straight through the open gate and into the house. Wolfe hurries in after him. Luckily Petra and Buffy are still upstairs. But Nothing has jumped onto the table in terror, her fur standing out like electrified soot, spitting ferociously. Potkins jumps around the table yapping, his claws scrabbling on the lino.

'Shhh,' says Wolfe, helplessly. Nothing chooses that moment of new-born panic to jump from the table and out of the open back door. 'Oh no . . .' Wolfe dives after her. Nothing is not allowed outside yet, not until she's had her injections, and now the dog is after her, looks as if he will eat her if Wolfe is not quick.

Nothing slips under the hedge and into Nell's garden. Kropotkin scratches at the earth under the hedge, trying to force himself through a little gap, his fat body wagging deliriously. Wolfe struggles to unlatch Nell's gate in order to get in and rescue the kitten before Kropotkin reaches her. But Nothing has already clambered up a bulging rubbish sack and onto Nell's kitchen window-sill, where Wolfe cannot quite reach her. There is a pane of glass missing from the window and Wolfe watches aghast as the kitten pushes herself through the sheet of plastic that has been Sellotaped over it. Her tail vanishes like a fluffy caterpillar, just as Kropotkin, with bits of stick stuck in his curly hair and his collar, bursts through the hedge.

'Oh no,' Wolfe mouths, staring at the window. He will have to get Nothing out or Buffy will go berserk. He does not want to see Nell, and he certainly doesn't want to see Rodney – not after letting him down yesterday – but there is nothing else he can do. He knocks at the door, timidly at first and then more loudly. He hears the kitten mewing in the kitchen, but apart from that the house is quiet. He waits a bit longer and then he goes to the funny curved shed and opens the door. Inside are a wheelbarrow, a rake, a pair of old boots and what he had hoped to find – a pair of step-ladders. He drags them out. They are old and heavy and the hinges creak when he opens them and he notices that the string is very frayed. He is terrified but he will be brave. The ladder wobbles with the stupid dog jumping round it and barking so loudly. 'Shhh,' he pleads again, and reaches over and gets his knee on the window-sill just as Kropotkin hurls his whole weight against the ladder, snapping the string and sending it crashing to the ground. Luckily, Wolfe is already half-way through the window. He pushes the sheet of polythene aside and the Sellotape tears from the frame and he is in, perched in the sink, his dirty shoes fizzing in some horrible bleachy stuff. He pulls out the plug and jumps down.

'Wolfe!' comes Petra's voice from outside. 'Whatever is going on?' He does not answer at once. He is in real trouble now, he knows it. He tiptoes out of the kitchen and into the dining-room searching for Nothing. The place is clean and cold and smells of swimming-pools.

'Wolfe! Are you all right? For goodness sake answer me!' He hears her trying the door.

'What are you doing?' cries Buffy. 'Where's Nothing? You left the door wide open and the gate . . . you just wait . . .'

Wolfe catches sight of Nothing hiding under the sideboard. He squats down and reaches for her and grasps her slight body and is so relieved to feel her cool live fur that he doesn't even care when her pinpoint teeth nip his thumb, and her claws catch in his skin. He carries Nothing to the door and tries it from the inside but it is locked with a key and the key is not there.

'Mum!' he shouts. 'I'm in here. I can't get out.' His voice
sounds very small and high-pitched in the lonely house.

'What on earth are you doing in there? Is anyone with you?'

'I came to rescue Nothing. Potkins was after her.' Buffy
gives a little scream. 'She's all right, Buff. I've got her, but I
can't get out. No one else is here. I got in through the window.'

'Can't you get back out of the window?' Petra asks. 'We'll
catch you if you can get back onto the sill.'

'No I can't . . . if I climb up I'll have to let go of Nothing.
Mum . . .' Wolfe begins to prickle with fear. The house is so
very quiet and so very cold. 'Get me out, Mum.'

'Have you tried the front door?' Petra asks. Wolfe tries it,
but as well as two separate locks and not a key to be seen, there
is a great big bolt right at the top.

'I'm looking for a key,' Petra calls. 'There must be a spare
key hidden somewhere . . .' her voice fades away a bit. 'I'm
looking in the shed,' she calls. 'It's an air-raid shelter,' she
explains to Buffy. 'I bet there's a key here somewhere . . . ah!
here we are. It's all right, Wolfe, I've found a key.'

Wolfe waits behind the door and listens to the key
scrabbling in the lock. He is scared to look behind him now.
What if Rodney is in the house, quietly listening to them?
What if he is behind him watching with cold and angry eyes?

'Quick, Mum,' he says. The kitten wriggles in his hands.
'Quick, Mum,' he says again, squirming with anxiety. He
needs a pee. The door opens suddenly inwards and Wolfe is
nearly knocked off his feet by an explosion of dog, as Potkins
bounds in and rushes around dementedly, knocking over
chairs, knocking over a tin bucket and a mop and then
charging up the stairs yapping furiously.

'Oh my God,' gasps Petra.

'Give me my cat,' Buffy demands. She snatches Nothing
from Wolfe's hands and stomps off back to their house.

'Are you all right, Wolfe?' Petra asks, hugging him briefly.

'Then go upstairs and chase the dog down again. I'll catch him. Hurry up. We'd better get out of here before anyone comes back. She'd go bonkers if she caught us in here.'

Wolfe clutches himself between his legs. He breathes in. And then he does what he's told, he follows Kropotkin up the stairs. The dog is barking and scratching at the door of a bedroom and he will not give up no matter how much Wolfe calls or pulls him by his collar. The only thing he can think of is to open the door and let the dog in so that he can chase him out and downstairs. The room is as cold as a fridge. The window is open to a rectangle of brilliant blue sky. The room is empty. Expect for a bed. Except for a bed with a man in it. A man with his head smashed in. Wolfe is frozen to the spot. The man's face is blue and there is money on his eyes. It is Rodney. Wolfe backs out of the room. Potkins skitters round the bare splintery floorboards, his breath leaving great doggy clouds in the clean air.

'Potkins!' calls Petra from the bottom of the stairs, 'here boy!' and the dog gives a yelp of excitement and hurls himself out past Wolfe and back down the stairs.

'Got him!' cries Petra. 'Come on, Wolfe . . . whatever are you doing up there?'

Wolfe shudders violently. Warm wetness creeps from between his clutching fingers. He quietly closes the door. He walks softly to the stairs. And then he rushes down as if there is a ghost behind him, panting down his neck.

'Mum!' he cries and throws himself at her.

'Whatever's the matter?' she asks, holding him against her with her free arm and then pushing him away. She is red-faced with the effort of holding onto Kropotkin's collar.

'I saw . . .' begins Wolfe and then stops. 'Nothing's the matter,' he says.

'Are you sure? What did you see?' Her face is creased with worry.

'It doesn't matter,' Wolfe says. The blue frozen man with the silver coins in his eyes is private. It is nothing to do with Wolfe, and nothing to do with Petra. It is horrible. There are horrible things going on here and the picture of Rodney will stay in his mind for ever. But they are going away. In a few hours they will be gone.

'Sure?'

'I'll take Potkins back,' Wolfe says.

'You look to me as if you need to use the toilet first,' Petra says, frowning at the wet patch on his trousers. 'Really Wolfie!'

'Sorry Mum,' says Wolfe.

*   *   *

Nell is scandalised by the state of Jim's allotment. She stands shaking her head at the weeds, at the frosted dying vegetables, and remembers the show-piece it used to be. 'I hardly like to get you out,' she says to Jim. 'Tragic, that's what I call it. A tragedy.'

'Don't fret,' replies the muffled voice of Jim. 'Times change.'

'But your lovely plot . . . rack and ruin. Now. I'm going to make you proud, Jim,' says Nell, setting the bag down and opening it to give him a bit of light. ' "Time to make your peace," you said, and you were right, Jim. I mean to make my peace today.'

'That's good to hear.'

'I'm going to dig up the cup, Jim, the silver prize cup that you buried for me. And I'm going to give it back.'

'You can't go digging. The ground must be like rock.'

'Don't worry, love. I know the spot. It's under the boundary and it's not very deep, only just under the turf. I'm not afraid of a spot of hard work in a good cause.'

Jim is silent in the handbag.

Nell looks at Arthur's plot. He hasn't made a bad job of it, considering. Kept it up all these years. Couldn't hold a candle to Jim's, as it was, of course. She chooses the spot where she remembers Jim telling her he buried the cup. She forces the prongs of the fork down with her boot. It is difficult make any impact at all at first, for the ground here is compact from years of being walked upon, and the frost has made it harder still. But Nell is nothing if not determined. 'Remember the war, Jim?' she says breathlessly, as she rests for a moment, one foot on the fork. 'How you said it was me, people like me, that kept up their standards in the war, people like me that were the backbone of Britain?' She presses all her weight on the fork. She has at last broken through the roots of the turf and now she peels it back to reveal the brown of the earth. 'Lipstick every day. Hitler had no effect on me!'

Once she is through the frosty top layer the going is easier, but still very hard work. Nell grows hot. She looks around, there's no one about to see, and she takes off her coat and folds it neatly beside her handbag. She swaps to the spade and a pile of earth soon grows beside her and she begins to perspire. This alarms her, the intimate trickling of it. She likes things cold and dry. But she will not give up now. It's deeper than she thought, but this is definitely the spot, one stride from the end of the boundary. Jim had pointed it out to her more than once. 'Safe as houses, Nell,' he'd said. And he is awfully quiet in the handbag.

* * *

Arthur enjoys his small freedom. Bless the lad for cheering Olive up with the hat so that he had been able to escape for a short stretch on the allotment. He breathes deeply. The sky is as clear and cold as a blue china bowl. The air invigorates. He stops at the top of the allotment looking down across the busy

patchwork of green and yellow, grey and brown, the ram-
shackle sheds, the rusting water-butts, to the busy flow of the
brown river below. His hand squeezes shut in his pocket. It
closes on emptiness, for of course the godstone is gone. 'Bless
the lad,' he murmurs.

*　*　*

'Ah,' says Nell. She is feeling dizzy now and the skin on her palms
burns. 'I think I've got it, Jim.' In the ground is a tin. It is an old
biscuit tin that she recognises from all that time ago, with a
picture of King George VI's coronation on the lid. She bends
down and reaches distastefully into the dirty hole. She has to
force her fingers down actually into the earth beside the tin in
order to ease it out. The earth gets between her fingers and under
her nails and under her wedding ring. She will not think of the
mindless seething of the soil, the seething spawning beasts upon
her skin. She will not think. She bites her lip in order not to think,
and tastes a bright bead of salty blood.

She sits down stiffly on her folded coat. Her head aches, and
her back, and her arms, and her palms smart. The tin opens
surprisingly easily. Inside is the cup. It is tarnished but it will
shine up a treat. She traces the inscription with her dirty finger.
It is a cheap thing, tawdry. To think she ever cared so much
about such a trifle!

Under the cup are other things. Old letters and photographs.
Puzzled, Nell lifts out the soft and slightly damp bundle and
unties the neat string bow. She sighs, remembering Jim's
neatness with knots and strings and so on. It is these little
things you forget. The string falls away. There is a photograph
of Olive. There is a photograph of Olive with an obscene smile
on her face, ear to ear, as if her face is about to split in two. The
smile is obscene and her bosom is uncovered. Nell suddenly
feels cold. The sweat hardens on her skin like crystals of frost.

'Jim,' she says. Olive's exposed bosom is large, her nipples huge and dark. Her eyes are bright, half-closed. She teases. 'Jim?' Jim always did love his photography, loved pottering about down in the cellar, evening after evening. She puts the photograph down and then she unfolds a letter. *My dearest Jim* it begins, and it is Olive's handwriting all right, messy and sprawling and loopy, Olive's handwriting all faded to brown on paper that is almost translucent with age, that feels like old skin. *My dearest Jim* it begins, and it is filthy. It goes on in a kind of exaggerated filthy way that is typical of Olive. Nell lets her eyes jitter over it quickly. She does not need to know the detail. There are words like 'ecstasy' and 'sex', there are words of the sort that no decent woman has any need to use. Nell screws it up. It is silent paper, as soft as skin in her hand. Nell closes her handbag with a snap, shutting Jim into its darkness.

There are other letters. There are other photographs. Nell does not wish to know any more, but one slips provokingly out of the bundle in her hand and as she snatches it up she cannot help but see. It is the two of them, Jim and Olive, together and they are grinning and . . . Nell breathes in sharply. Olive is expecting and Jim has his hand on her belly just like the father, just as if he is the proud father of her baby. Nell's heart struggles violently against her ribs. But it was Arthur's child, the one that died, it was Arthur and Olive's. She had had only one child and it was Arthur's. It was not Jim's, never Jim's, could not have been. She stands up. She looks this way and that, turns about as if searching for something, looks wildly around her but there is no help to be had.

She feels that she is slipping again, losing control. She clutches the handle of the spade and closes her eyes and her father's face looms suddenly in front of her, and she sees his disdain. His mouth is drawn into a tight pucker as if with a wire, and his brow lowers like a storm-cloud. It is as if he always knew. He always knew she had it in her, beneath the china-doll exterior, she always had it in her to kill. She tried so hard to be a perfect girl. She fitted the mould around her snug as a pink and white porcelain shell. But now the mould had shattered. From inside it has shattered with the force of her rage and she stands loose and light, insubstantial. She shivers, and yet strangely it is heat she feels rather than cold on this frosty morning. She opens her eyes and dispels, once and for all, her father's disdain. She is all rage, all surging glorious rage. The shards of her shell lie scattered all around her on the earth and the sun glints upon them.

She opens her handbag again and takes Jim out. 'Nell?' he says, his voice puzzled, as if recognition is gone. She tries to look at him but all there is is the brightness of the sky reflected in the glass, and the reflection of her own wild strange face. 'Nell?' the voice is faint. She picks up the letters and the photographs and throws them in the hole. She flings Jim in after them, and then the cup. Olive's prize lands with a clunk, as if there is something else buried there, not far down, some metal thing. Nell peers into the earth. She can see nothing at first, just the stony earth. She grits her teeth and grips the handle of the spade between her burning hands. If there is something else, she might just as well know what it is.

*   *   *

Arthur squints. Surely it's a trick of the light. It looks as if there is someone on his plot, someone digging on his plot – no, Jim's plot – no, the boundary. It is a tall grey-haired person: a woman. It looks like . . . no, surely it can't be . . . it looks just like Nell. She is bending over a hole. And it is Nell. Arthur will not approach. He will let her be. There is something wild about the way her head is jutting forward, the way she jerks the spade, and he will not encroach upon her trouble. He stands at the top of the slope and watches her lift the spade.

* * *

Something that is not blood, that is more like quicksilver than blood, rushes through Nell's veins. The energy that surges through her arms is terrific. It feels as if one jump is all that it would take to soar. In her mind fly balsa planes and cups and hats and perhaps it is madness but she doesn't care. The smarting of her hands is wonderful. She rips the wedding ring from her finger and flings it into the hole and laughs at the cheap chink it makes against Olive's cup. Jim lies in the earth, and his glass is cracked. He reflects the sun at her in sharp flakes and the brightness makes her blink and squint, makes her eyes water. There he lies in the earth and his cracked glassy face merges for a moment with that of her father, with Rodney. He lies in the earth. It is about time.

She scrapes the soil from the buried thing but she still cannot see. The sun reflecting from Jim's glass gets into her eyes and she cannot see. She lifts her spade to give it a whack. It is old and metal. She blinks. It is a blunt-nosed thing. She lets her spade fall and as it falls she realises what it is. It is a bomb, of course, left over from the war.

* * *

There is not much left when Arthur gets there. And there are soon people swarming: police, Army, the press. He stands back. His allotment is in ruins. Everything vanished into the crater, all the lovely seedlings, all the roots, everything. His hand in his pocket is empty. Yes, the godstone is gone. All those years, is all he can think, all that time, all the lovely earth and what was buried there all that time . . .

* * *

On Remembrance Sunday, while the bells toll and people wear their scarlet poppies to church, Arthur takes Kropotkin to the allotments for a walk, for a snuffle in the winter earth. All the fuss is over by now. The allotments stand empty and cold. Arthur finds a scrap of a photograph. It is old and faded and dampened by the rain and muddied by the soil. It is a photograph of a young couple and the man is Jim in his uniform, and the woman is smudged and torn. He can see that she is pregnant, though he cannot see her face, but of course, it is poor Nell. He screws it up and throws it down. He gives Kropotkin a tug. Olive will be waiting for him in her lipstick and her cherry hat, and they'll shuffle up to the Lamb for a glass of stout before their dinner. And that will be a pleasure. The sound of the river hurrying over the stones is loud. Arthur gazes down at the park, at a boy on a bicycle, and he thinks of Wolfe. He thinks of the godstone in Wolfe's pocket all that way away, working its magic for the planting of his tree.

A NOTE ON THE AUTHOR

Lesley Glaister was born in Wellingborough. She teaches a Master's Degree in Writing at Sheffield Hallam University. She is the author of the novels *Honour Thy Father*, which won the Somerset Maugham and a Betty Trask award, *Digging to Australia*, *Limestone and Clay*, *Partial Eclipse*, *The Private Parts of Women*, *Easy Peasy*, *Sheer Blue Bliss* and *Now You See Me*. She lives in Sheffield.